Treasure on Jekyll

GEM OF THE GOLDEN ISLES SERIES
BOOK THREE

BEACH HOUSE
PUBLISHING

Treasure on Jekyll

GEM OF THE GOLDEN ISLES SERIES BOOK THREE

SANDY MALONE

BEACH HOUSE PUBLISHING

Beach House Publishing

544 Old Plantation Road

Jekyll Island

ISBN: 979-8-9901756-5-5 (paperback)

ISBN: 979-8-9901756-4-8 (ebook)

Library of Congress Control Number:2024906160

Cover design by: Patricia Tait

Printed in the United States of America

Disclaimer

This is a work of fiction. Unless indicated below, all the names, characters, brides, grooms, businesses, places, events, venues, and incidents in this book are either the product of the author's imagination or used in a fictitious manner. Any resemblance to actual persons, living or dead, or actual events is purely coincidental.

There are a number of real Jekyll residents and businesses featured; however, their roles in the book are fictional. Their names have been used with their permission. The author recommends every business mentioned.

The annual Island Treasures hide-and-seek hunt has very specific rules and parameters which the author completely ignored when creating the game for a wedding group. Please refer to the proper guidelines, which an be found through Jekyll Island Authority website at https://www.jekyllisland.com/signature-events/island-treasures/.

Finally, the end of the book does cross into the beginning of the pandemic, and the author chose to ignore that fact.

Dedication

Treasure on Jekyll is dedicated to the brides who trusted me with their wedding plans, and the interns who helped us make their dreams come true.

Some of you became besties, some of you had me on your push lists when you gave birth, and a few reached out to have their wedding videos taken down after the union dissolved. I feel like I've lived vicariously through you. Which is amazing because I think most destination wedding planners wonder about what ever happened to the couples they married. Thank you for keeping me in the loop.

I couldn't have planned all those weddings without the help of the interns who rotated through our Vieques office over the years. Some of you stayed until you burned out (Kelsi Welch) and some of you went on to bigger and better careers in event planning (Kayla Blunk). But all of you have become amazing women with great lives and I couldn't be prouder of you or more grateful for your help. I love all of you.

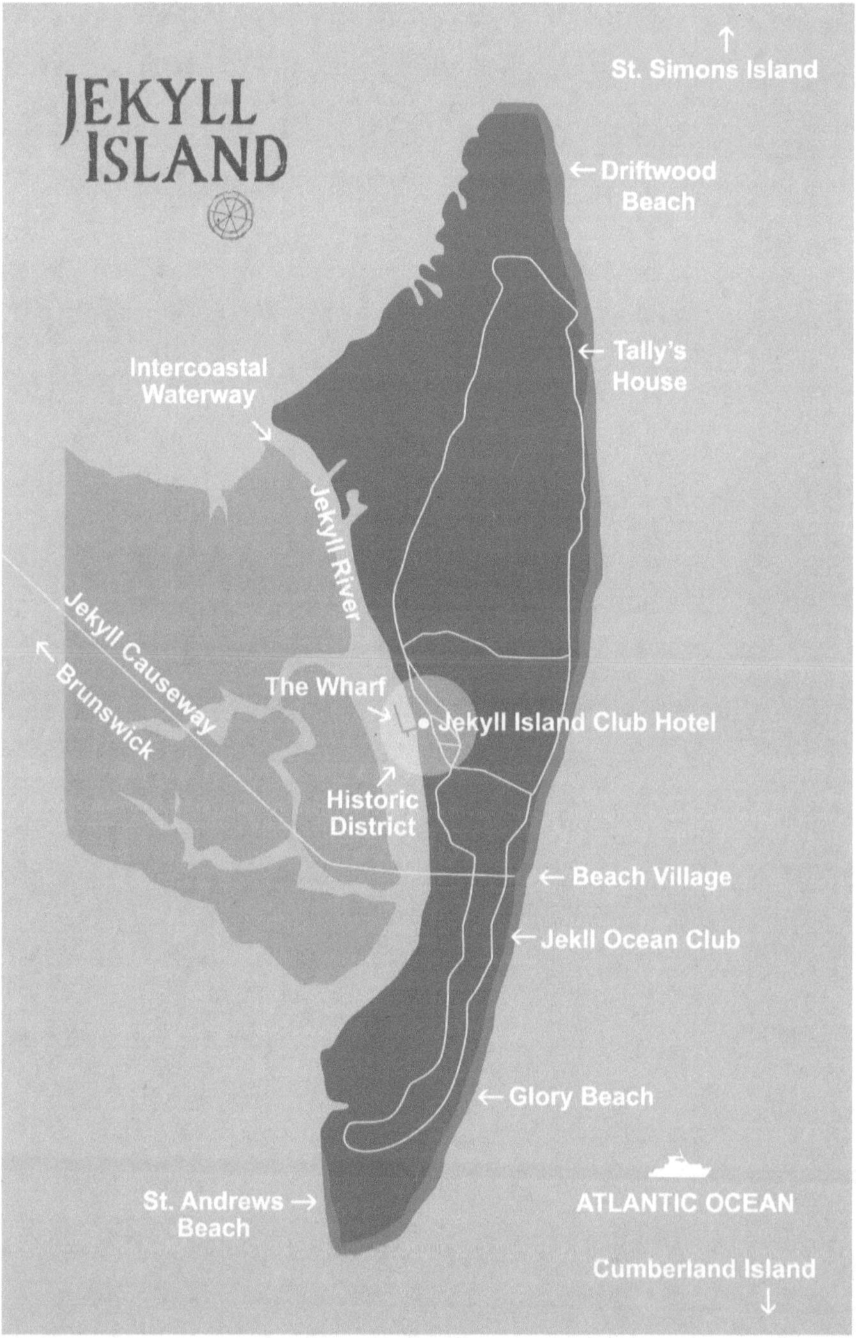

JEKYLL ISLAND
St. Simons Island
Driftwood Beach
Tally's House
Intercoastal Waterway
Jekyll River
Jekyll Causeway
Brunswick
The Wharf
Jekyll Island Club Hotel
Historic District
Beach Village
Jekll Ocean Club
Glory Beach
St. Andrews Beach
ATLANTIC OCEAN
Cumberland Island

Chapter 1

November 2019

Tally sat in the back of the historic chapel watching Kayla run the rehearsal, and wondered, not for the first time, what these sisters had been thinking when they'd decided to have a double wedding. They appeared to hate each other. They had argued over absolutely everything from the first moment the wedding planner met them when they came to look at venues on Jekyll Island.

At this moment, they were arguing over which couple was going to do their vows first. This decision had already been made, two or three times, if Tally remembered correctly. But apparently, none of those previous decisions had stuck. And now the entire wedding party was getting involved. She watched Kayla try to shout over them for a minute before she went to her rescue.

"Hey! People! People!" Tally yelled, using a softer voice with each word, once she got their attention. "We are inside a beautiful and historic chapel that has withstood the test of time for more than 100 years. Let's all adjust our voices and attitudes to show the proper respect to the chapel and to each other." She was using a regular speaking voice by the time she finished.

"Alrighty, everybody who is not a bride or a groom, please take a seat," she pointed to the pews. "You can stay," she told the minister in a joking tone.

Tally had worked with the nondenominational officiant countless times and knew the pastor was probably laughing in her head. But she kept her face appropriately solemn while Tally took control of the situation. The brides' and grooms' parents were already seated in the front pews of the chapel, watching, but not involving themselves in the bruhaha.

"Okay, now, does either of you care which couple exchanges vows first, dances first, or does the toasts first, etc.?" Tally asked both of the grooms, who were standing together as far away as they could reasonably get from the women they were about to marry.

Both men shook their heads, and she thought she heard one of them say "no," but she couldn't be certain. Neither of them would make eye contact with his fiancée. So Tally went with it.

"Nope? Okay, perfect. You two can sit down now, too," she was using a cross between her kindergarten teacher voice and her high school gym teacher voice. And it was working. Both grooms looked relieved to have been taken off the hot seat as they slid into the pews by their parents.

She turned to face the root of the problem and found both brides glaring at her.

Tally took a deep breath and smiled before she began talking. *Woosah,* she thought, *woosah.*

"We have talked about this ad nauseum, ladies. And it's been sorted out more than once. I propose that we go with the order of everything as it currently appears on the final schedule that you approved a week ago."

Both women began talking at the same time, and Tally held up a hand to silence them.

"After you *both* approved the final schedule for the weekend, we sent it to each individual vendor and confirmed they had read and understood it," Tally continued. "It's too late to keep switching things around. Something isn't going to happen when you want it to happen if you change things at the eleventh hour.

"Let's review what we all agreed to and see if we can live with it," Tally looked over at the girls' mother for some reinforcement and saw that the woman who had spawned these brides was scrolling through her phone, ignoring it all. Fabulous. Their father sat in the first pew looking like he would rather be anywhere else.

Tally looked at her clipboard to refresh her memory. Kayla had been dealing with the crazy sisters for most of the planning because they gave her boss a headache, but it was only two days into the four-day wedding weekend and the brides had already broken their wedding planner. Tally had never seen her friend Kayla Hendrix look so completely defeated. It would be funny if it weren't tragic – she remembered feeling that way for a couple of especially awful weddings she'd planned her first year on Vieques Island, Puerto Rico. But she'd never planned a double wedding before.

The 31-year-old wedding planner had been excited at first when one of the girls – she didn't remember which one – inquired about double weddings on Jekyll. Something as unusual as that would be a lot of fun and make amazing pictures for the Jekyll Weddings website. Social media loved her clients, the nuttier the better. As long as the wedding was gorgeous, and the crazy was posted by the bride and her friends first, Tally couldn't help sharing, too. A lot of her weddings went viral.

Tally had been excited to meet the Beauregard sisters when they came to visit Jekyll Island to look at venues with their mother. Her initial form to set up the free consultation didn't ask for a lot of personal details, although many potential clients chose to share everything but their bra size in the section that asked if they wanted to include additional information. The Beauregards' inquiry had been rather generic, with just the preferred date, number of guests, and a short note. It was the note that intrigued her.

"This is a double wedding and the brides are sisters."

The women standing in front of her looked alike. So much so that, right off the bat, Tally asked them if they were twins.

Both women flushed, looked horrified, and then simultaneously spat the word "NO" at her so venomously that she was pretty certain she had just blown getting hired.

She wanted to make a run for it, but instead, she took a deep breath and said, "Well, that's awkward. How about let's start over again. I'm Tally and it's nice to meet you. Which of you is older?" she asked, extending her hand to the sister standing closest to her.

The woman paused for a second before accepting Tally's hand with a limp-fish handshake and a clammy paw that made Tally want to wipe her hands on her pants. But she resisted the urge.

"I'm the eldest," she told Tally as she let go of her hand. "My name is Pamela Louise Beauregard, and I got engaged first." She made the statement like it was a very important fact for Tally to remember. She made a mental note as she reached out to shake the other bride's hand.

"And so, you must be Penelope?" she smiled at the other sister.

"Penelope Lavergne Beauregard," the woman corrected Tally in a tone that made their wedding planner wonder if she was supposed to use all three names to address them at all times. She noticed they had the same initials and made another note to explore that as a décor option.

Their mother was wandering around the Boar's Head Lounge of the historic Jekyll Island Club Hotel, looking at the pictures on the wall and taking in the décor. But she didn't engage with her daughters and their potential wedding planner at all. Tally had to walk over to her and get her attention to introduce herself after one of the sisters – who knew which was which – pointed out the mother of the bride.

Both of the brides wore their dark red hair – the kind that could only be natural – long and blown-out straight. Pamela wore hers down and Penelope had it clipped back in a barrette. They both had the kind of creamy porcelain skin that made Tally jealous, and deep blue eyes that made her do a double-take. They were wearing similar outfits in two different colors. Pamela's skirt and jacket were blue, and Penelope's dress and jacket were lavender. The light-purple suit was double-breasted but Tally was pretty sure they'd both been made by the same designer.

The women were a year apart in age and had been best friends and worst enemies all their lives, she later learned. People probably assumed Pamela and Penelope were twins because that's how they acted – as little girls, they'd even made up their own language. But as much as they loved each other, they fought even harder. And Tally had picked up on that from the start.

She walked them around the Grand Dining Room, where the Astors, Rockefellers, and Goodyears had celebrated occasions, and then they got coffees and found seats on the porch of the hotel so they could talk wedding details.

"Why are you having a double wedding?" Tally asked. "You seem to have vastly different ideas about what you want for big days."

"Because our father is cheap," Penelope snapped.

Tally had to use some serious self-control not to burst out laughing. It was obvious to anyone who met these sisters that their father was anything but cheap. From Penelope's big Louis Vuitton purse to the red bottoms of Pamela's Louboutin pumps, nothing about the women was inexpensive.

"So, your father wants you to get married together, but you don't want to share a wedding?" she was confused and wanted to get it sorted before they went any farther in the planning process.

The girls' mother, who hadn't said more than three words up to that point, suddenly engaged.

"He's not cheap, girls. He's thrifty," she said as if it was a phrase she repeated regularly. "Their father will throw them each their own big, gorgeous wedding, but not in the same year. If Penelope and Pamela both want to get married in the same 12 months, he can't see the point in doing the two separately for what will mostly be the same group of wedding guests. The grooms have been friends for years, too. Our daughters have done everything together their whole lives and, in my husband's opinion, having two weddings, one after the other, feels redundant."

Tally didn't agree, because she knew that few brides would want to give up half the attention at the wedding to another woman in white. But Mrs. Beauregard wasn't asking for Tally's opinion. She was explaining why things were the way they were.

"I got engaged first," Pamela reminded them.

"Duly noted," Tally said, and then wished she hadn't.

"But I've been together with Barry for longer." Penelope actually stood up and put her hands on her hips as she made her point. Her mother reached for her younger daughter's hand and gently tugged her back into her seat.

And that was how all of the planning went. If Pamela chose pink napkins, her sister wanted green. Penelope wanted to get married on the beach, but Pamela preferred Faith Chapel. For many things – like the bouquets – it was fine that the women had vastly different taste. There was no reason for them to carry the same flowers, have similar dresses, or use the same vows. They would have two wedding cakes so that both couples could get cake cutting pictures and have their own favorite flavors. They could have two favor tables. However, some details that they had to pick together – like music and décor – required a lot of compromise and all of their wedding planner's patience.

Tally didn't meet the brides' father in person until the wedding weekend, but she'd found Mr. Beauregard to be quick to send payments when she emailed invoices to him. Only once did he question her judgement enough to pick up the telephone and call. He wanted her to explain why he'd received two bills for wedding photography deposits.

"We need two photographers for everything," Tally explained. "The girls are dressing in two different suites, and both want pictures of the process. They could not agree on a favorite photographer, so they each got their own. It's not a lot more money than using the same company with more cameras, and so I didn't think it was worth the argument with the brides. We don't want the photographer to miss an important moment with Penelope and Barry because they were busy shooting a picture of Pamela and Trevor."

It must have made sense to her clients' father because he thanked her and ended the call. She received two deposit checks for the photogs via Priority Mail a couple of days later.

Every planning call had been a struggle, with Penelope and Pamela arguing about the minutia, like signature cocktail names and the color of their monogram on the cocktail napkins, rather than focusing on the big picture. She hadn't seen either brides' dress because they were both keeping them hidden under super-secret lock and key until the wedding day. They hadn't even shown them to each other.

Tally and Kayla had expected things to get easier after all of the vendors were booked, but they hadn't accounted for the competitive nature of the Beauregard sisters. They fought over whose name would be first on the wedding invitations, who would go down the aisle first, who would say "I do" first, who would be introduced at the reception first, and who would start off the first dances. More than once, Tally asked them to table their arguments for after the planning call – it was a waste of time and they didn't need her to help them fight – and moved on to the next item on her list, hoping it would get them off the struggle bus. Kayla had participated in all of the planning with the sisters and after one particularly miserable conference call, she offered to take the Beauregards off Tally's hands.

"I've never done a double wedding and I'd be nervous, so how about you run it and I act as your second through the remainder of the process? I think two brides calls for two wedding planners – especially with sisters as high-maintenance as these 'young ladies.' And I do use that term loosely here," Tally said. She was happy to have Kayla field the brides' endless emails, texts, and calls.

The final schedule that the sisters had eventually, and begrudgingly, approved with Kayla had them going down the aisle together, on both sides of their father. Pamela and Trevor and their wedding party would be on the left side of the altar, and Penelope and Barry's attendants would be with them on the right.

Some pieces of the ceremony had naturally been combined. The minister had asked "who gives these women" instead of "this woman," and Mr. Beauregard only had to stand up once give both of his daughters away.

Tally had made the girls choose an order for the officiant to follow throughout the entire ceremony, because switching around who went first for what was too confusing for the minister and the guests. Pamela was older and came first alphabetically, so Tally proposed that she go first for everything at the wedding ceremony.

"She'll be married a minute ahead of you, Penelope," Tally explained. "And that just sort of seems right because she's traditionally done things first. But we'll switch it up and go the other direction for the reception."

The smug smile on Pamela's face disappeared. "Please explain how that will work," she said.

"I think you girls should make your entrance together at the reception with your new husbands. It tracks because you went down the aisle together," Tally began. "But then, Penelope and Barry will have the first dance and yours with Trevor will be next.

"We'll do the all the toasts for one couple, then all the toasts for the other couple. Please cross-check your lists. Anybody who is on both lists – your parents, grandparents, etc. – can give one toast for both couples unless there's a special reason to do them separately. We need to keep things moving because toasts can drag when you only have one bride and groom. The longer they sit, the less you all get to dance," she reminded them.

All the arguing and negotiating and compromising had meant absolutely nothing, Tally realized at the wedding rehearsal. The sisters just liked to argue about everything, regardless of how unpleasant it was for everyone who had to watch them. The nonchalant attitudes of the bridesmaids and groomsmen led Tally and Kayla to believe that this was normal behavior for "the Ps," as they'd taken to calling the sisters around their office.

The rehearsal had dissolved into chaos and Tally clapped her hands to get their attention, again.

"Okay, let's do this the way it was written. I don't care who won Rock-Paper-Scissors last night," she said. She couldn't even look at Kayla as she said it, because she'd definitely start laughing. "We're going to go with what's on the schedule that you guys approved last week. No changes."

Something in her tone must've alerted the brides because they stopped arguing with her, even if they continued to bicker with each other. And they got through the rest of the rehearsal.

Chapter 2

Pamela and Penelope were better behaved after the rehearsal fiasco, and the dinner given by the grooms' parents later that evening was a resounding success. Tally slept late the next morning and worked from home, with a plan to be on hand at the ceremony and reception in case Kayla needed her to referee. She was leaving the day-of setup in the younger planner's capable hands. Unless something went terribly wrong, she wouldn't be needed until mid-afternoon.

So of course, Kayla called mid-morning while Tally and her fiancé, Mitch Durham, were drinking coffee on the front deck of their beach house. Tally grew up in the waterfront home overlooking the Atlantic Ocean. Her Aunt Etah, who'd built the house on Jekyll Island nearly 50 years ago, had given it to the couple as an early wedding gift.

"What's up, buttercup?" Tally answered.

"I think we might have a problem," Kayla whispered. "I need you to look at something."

"What?"

"I'm sending you pictures now," Kayla said.

The morning sun on the front deck made it impossible for Tally to see the screen on her phone. She got up to walk into the house, and then put the phone on speaker so she could check her texts.

She looked at the first picture Kayla had sent, and then the second. Then she went back to the first one again.

"No fucking way."

"Way," Kayla replied.

"Is it really the exact same dress?" Tally asked.

"Not exactly the same. Penelope's is white and Pamela's is ivory."

"And nobody knew about this?"

"Nope. You know how they were all super-secret about everything? I think when they learned the dresses weren't the same color, they didn't exchange any other details. Their mom mentioned last night that she was looking forward to seeing them, so I don't think she has the slightest idea," Kayla said. "This is going to be bad."

"Oh boy," Tally sighed. "They're not doing formal pre-ceremony pictures so they won't know about this until they see each other after they do the first-look pictures with their grooms. We're going to have a total meltdown right before they're supposed to go down the aisle."

"I want to run away," Kayla whispered. She wasn't kidding.

"Me too."

They were both quiet for a second, and then Tally spoke up.

"Okay, well this is not our mistake. This is entirely on them. And their parents know it. We can both make sure to mention to some of the guests how excited we were to see their dresses revealed, too, just in case anybody thinks we knew and didn't do anything to prevent the duplication."

"OMG we asked them to send us pictures of their dresses on every conference call. They didn't trust us not to 'leak' it," Kayla ranted.

"But we can't tell people that," her boss said. "Do you want me to come over there earlier than we'd planned?"

"No, I guess not. Not at this point. Everything is on track. The girls are at breakfast," Kayla reported. "The boys are playing golf. The Ps actually followed our instructions and hung their gowns out in their suites last night, and that's how I noticed the problem."

"Okay, well don't say anything to anyone about it just yet. There's zero crossover between the two bridal suites so if we're careful, the world won't end while they're getting hair and makeup done. I'll call both of the photographers and give them a heads up. There's no way they won't say something the second they notice if I don't warn them."

"This is going to be the longest day ever," Kayla whined.

"Yep."

Tally hung up the phone and went back outside to the deck.

"What was the problem?" Mitch asked.

"The psycho sisters bought the exact same wedding dress, and we're the only ones who know it."

"What the..." he began. Then he started laughing.

"I know, I know. I couldn't make this nonsense up if I tried." She put her face in her hands and started laughing.

"Are you going to warn them?" he asked, as he looked at the pictures on the phone Tally handed him.

"Nope." She stopped laughing.

"Seriously?" his eyes widened.

"It's too late to do anything about it. Better to have them freak for 30 seconds before I shove them down the aisle than to have them getting hysterical all afternoon," Tally explained. "I'll probably warn their dad, just so he's prepared to drag them if necessary."

"Wow. You're going to have fun blogging about this wedding," he joked.

"It's a therapeutic way to cope with wedding planning trauma," she said defensively. "Otherwise, I'd have to drink more."

They couple talked about their plans for Tuesday – Tally's only day off most weeks – when they were supposed to start working on their own wedding planning, and Mitch suggested they do it on the beach if the weather was good. His dark, thick hair was a mess – he still had bedhead – and he hadn't shaved. But he was still the hottest guy she'd ever dated, even as he sat there in his Georgia Bulldogs boxer shorts.

A moment later, she got up from her chair and walked over to her fiancé. She bent over to plant a kiss on his lips and he pulled her into his lap. Tally knew she had to put an end to their canoodling if she was going to get anything done.

"I need to go get dressed. I know Kayla said she didn't need me, but she was lying," she told Mitch. "She just doesn't want to bother me."

"Probably," he agreed, and pushed her out of his lap and onto her feet.

"If I'm here dying just thinking about this, she's gotta be in worse shape, standing there looking at those dresses." Tally chuckled for a second. "I'm going to shower now and get my act together so I can go play wing-woman. A double wedding apparently requires two planners on site all day on the day of. Note to self."

Chapter 3

When Tally arrived at the hotel, she ran into the wedding photographers in the lobby. They were on their way up to the bridal suites, and Tally joined them. It was impossible to avoid joking about what they were walking into, but before they got off the elevator, Tally reminded both of the teams that they had to keep it together or things would quickly spin out of control. The dress fiasco couldn't be fixed but the blow-up over it could be delayed and mitigated.

Tally went to Penelope's room first because she was the less frightening of the Beauregard sisters. The bride was in a chair having her hair done and the wedding gown was hanging in the wide doorway between the bedroom and the living room.

"Happy wedding day!" she greeted her client with a big smile and real enthusiasm. "Are you so excited?"

"I am, I am," Penelope said, grinning ear to ear. "Do you like my dress?"

"It's absolutely beautiful," Tally said. "You're going to look amazing in it. You have such gorgeous hair and eyes – you could have worn a trash bag and looked fantastic. That gown is just the cherry on top." She told all of her brides the same thing in one form or another.

She introduced Penelope to her photographers.

"I'm going to check on Pamela and then I'll be back to see how things are going here. Do you need anything?" Tally asked the bride.

"Nothing I can think of. Thank you for asking. My bridesmaids are taking excellent care of me," Penelope said.

"Great. Well, we're nearby if you need us so just text." Then Tally scooted out the door of the bridal suite before anybody could stop her to ask a question. Kayla was right behind.

"Okay let's go see Pamela now," Tally said.

"Do I have to?" Kayla asked in a joking tone. "She woke up on the wrong side of the bed."

"Ew. Yes, I need backup. She scares me."

"She scares me more."

Pamela had woken up in a foul mood on her wedding day and had taken it out on everybody around her. They could hear her snapping at somebody from the hallway as they approached the bridal suite's door. Tally took a deep breath and then walked in.

"Happy wedding day!" Tally called as they entered the suite. "Oh wow, Pamela. You look gorgeous!"

The bride's hair was already done, swept into a fancy updo with a tiara that had a hook for her veil. She was sitting in the makeup chair scowling, looking very much the same - and yet, the polar-opposite - as her sister, just one floor beneath them.

"I didn't sleep well at all," Pamela griped. "And I don't think dinner agreed with me either. I've got a headache and the hairdresser made it worse by poking me with all the bobby pins."

"I'm sorry," Tally tried to sound genuine. "But the final result is terrific. And it'll probably hold up all night if she's got so many pins in it. No pain, no gain, right? It hurts to be the perfect bride."

Pamela didn't laugh, but the sour look on her face softened a little bit.

"What do you think of my gown?" she asked her wedding planner.

Tally turned to look around the room for Pamela's dress. The maid of honor pointed to the corner where the hanger was hooked on a piece of art on the wall. She inwardly cringed but didn't say anything. Instead, she reached over and carefully lifted the hangar.

"Let's hang this in a doorway so we can spread out that fabulous train," she suggested and didn't wait for approval. "This dress is gorgeous. I love the ivory satin. It's almost a champagne color. Very posh looking."

"I got it in a shop in Manhattan," Pamela announced, as if the only pretty wedding gowns in the world were in New York City.

Tally said nothing but smiled and nodded.

The dress was strapless. There were handstitched beaded flowers on the bodice that seemed to float into nothing as they traveled down the gown. It was the exact same dress her younger sister was wearing, except the beading on Pamela's was done with gold thread to go with her ivory silk, and Penelope's beading had silver thread against her bright white silk.

"All of the bridesmaid dresses came from the same place as my gown," Pamela continued. "It took a lot of time for everybody to go up and do their fittings, but I think they'll see it was worth it."

Her bridesmaids were wearing floor-length, sleeveless, orchid dresses that flattered none of them. Tally wondered if her client had chosen them intentionally. She seemed like the type who would want to ensure nobody looked as good as she did on her wedding day.

"I love that color," the wedding planner lied with a smile.

When none of the bridesmaids spoke up to agree with her, Tally figured there was some consternation surrounding the dress shopping and quickly moved the topic along to bouquets. At least those would be dramatically different. Pamela was carrying stems of big white calla lilies while Penelope had chosen pink oriental lilies. All of the bridesmaids' bouquets were made of a combination of the two flowers, but using mini calla lilies, and all of the grooms were getting miniature calla lily boutonnieres.

The subject of flowers made Pamela smile, almost.

"I love my bouquet," she admitted. "It's exactly what I wanted." She gestured toward a row of cylinder vases lined up on the windowsill. Each vase held one perfect bouquet.

"Good, I'll tell my team."

"It looks just like the picture I sent you," Pamela said, sounding surprised.

"That's what we were supposed to do. I'm so happy that you're pleased. I think you're going to be a stunning bride," Tally said. She started to add "and so is your sister," but she thought better of it and stopped herself. If Pamela wanted to hear about Penelope today, she probably would have gotten ready with her.

Tally and Kayla escaped Pamela's suite as fast as they could.

"Oh. My. God." Tally said after they'd gotten away from the door. "It's literally the exact same designer in two different shades of satin." They were pricey dresses and they'd been custom-made for the sisters. How did the company not see they'd sold two of the same dresses to two brides named Beauregard in the same state? Just thinking about it made her brain hurt.

"I know. I can't even believe this," Kayla agreed.

"How is everything else going?" Tally asked, not really wanting to know the answer but needing to change the subject.

"Actually, everybody else is pretty happy," the young planner reported with a toss of her long, blonde ponytail. "The guys had lunch at Tribuzio's Grille after golf – turns out that Trevor and Barry were in the same fraternity at Chapel Hill and all of the groomsmen already knew each other. They've been really easy since they arrived," Kayla reported.

"Have all of the vendors checked in?"

"Everything is here except the cakes, and they're not due to be delivered for another hour. The band and the DJ did their setup and sound check as soon as we got the room. Bouquets are in the brides' rooms and I brought the reception centerpieces with me. Oh, and Yaya is decorating the chapel." Kayla scanned her list.

"I've already done the placecards and the table numbers, but you could do a loop around them and proof my work. I was going pretty fast," Kayla explained.

"I can do that," Tally made a note on her own clipboard. They always double-checked the placecards.

"We still need to put out the favors but I wasn't sure we'd ever settled that debate. Are we putting them on the tables or by the exit?" Kayla asked.

Tally groaned. It had been yet another stupid sticking point. The sisters didn't seem to get that they had to do one or the other, or have twice as many favors, because guests would see two different things and think they were supposed to get both.

"I wouldn't say it was settled but I put my foot down. We're going to do favor tables on both sides of the doorway with a picture of the right couple on that table," she told Kayla. "If we put all the favors on the dinner tables, and give family members and close friends one of each like the girls want, there won't be any room left for centerpieces. I'm making an executive decision on this one. Besides," she said with a snicker. "Ain't nobody gonna be complaining about favors after they get a load of each other's dresses."

"How can you laugh about this, Tally?" Kally looked appalled.

"Years of experience. There's no crying in wedding planning. In situations like this, we just have to laugh and hope everybody else does, too."

"I don't think Pamela and Penelope are going to laugh."

"Neither do I. But getting myself worked up about it isn't going to help. I'd rather practice primal scream therapy. But I can't do that when I'm standing in a hotel hallway, so instead, I laugh," Tally said logically.

Chapter 4

As predicted, Penelope and Pamela did not laugh when they saw each other just outside the entrance to Faith Chapel. The beautiful interdenominational chapel was built for the members of the Jekyll Island Club in 1904. It replaced Union Chapel, which had been moved to a different spot to be used for worship by the African-American employees on the island.

The shrieks that erupted from both brides when they saw each other rattled the structure's 100-year-old Tiffany stained-glass window dedicated to the memory of the Singer Sewing machine founder and signed by "Louis C. Tiffany, NY."

Tally had wisely shut the doors to the chapel and made sure the music was going full volume before the sisters saw each other. The music had been their father's suggestion. Mr. Beauregard had known that his daughters would scream bloody murder when they saw each other in the same dress.

"I'm so sorry about this," Tally had said when she told him about it. "I had no idea."

Mr. Beauregard started laughing.

"My girls have always been very, very similar, and they hate it," he ex-plained. "They look the same, they sound the same. Even when they try not to. More than once, they would arrive home for the holidays - from colleges in totally different states, mind you - and both would have changed their hair to the exact same new hairdo without having discussed it. The summer Pam went to Paris and Pen went to Los Angeles, they both came home with short, blond hair. Go figure."

Tally was glad the father of the brides could laugh about it. Their mother was there when Tally gave him the news, but Mrs. Beauregard was checked-out as usual. She literally had no reaction to the news that her daughters had accidentally duplicated their wedding gowns. The wedding planners had decided she was a heavily-medicated woman based on their few interactions with her. But they were shocked she didn't have anything to say about her daughters' dress fiasco.

"Can I have some of what she's on?" Kayla whispered and Tally made a face before looking away so she didn't start laughing.

"If I may make a suggestion," Mr. Beauregard said. "Be sure to have somebody standing in between the girls when they see each other so it doesn't turn physical. It wouldn't be the first time those two have gone to church covered in grass stains from fighting on the way in."

"Duly noted," Tally said, hoping that he was exaggerating. There was no way she was going to get in the middle of that catfight.

"Do you think we should warn Barry and Trevor?" Kayla asked.

"The grooms?" Tally asked incredulously, and a little too loudly. "I will make a money bet with you right now that they won't notice the wedding gowns are the same until their brides start bitching about it to them."

"Ha! Don't make that bet," the father-of-the-brides advised Kayla. "My future sons-in-law might not even notice if we switched up the girls." Mr. Beauregard laughed heartily at that, and the wedding planners giggled with him. But as soon as he turned away from them, Tally and Kayla exchanged a look of horror.

Chapter 5

"No she didn't," Mitch thought Tally was kidding when she told him all about it late that night.

"Oh yes, she did. Pamela took that big fat calla lily bouquet and whomped Penelope in the head with it. A few times," Tally started laughing again and had to take a breath to continue the story. "When a few of the blooms broke off and hit the ground, I think it dawned on her what she was doing so she stopped. But she'd already wrecked her sister's hair and destroyed her own bouquet."

"Wow."

"Yeah, that's when their father stepped in and told them to stop the nonsense. I was just going to let them fight it out. Kayla was filming in case we need it for insurance later." Tally was dead serious.

"Did they listen to him?" Mitch asked, wanting to hear the end of the story.

"Not at first. But then he threatened to deduct the cost of their wedding from their trust funds if they didn't act like adults. He basically ordered them to pull up their big girl panties and they did it," she said.

"Thank God, Yaya was still there when the shit hit the fan," Tally continued. "She fixed Penelope's hair while I made a new bouquet for Pamela out of the leftovers. Funny thing is that she ended up with a bouquet identical to Penelope's because she ruined her own. Karma gave her exactly what she didn't want. Funny how that works.

"When they calmed down a bit, I suggested they should pretend they had bought the same dress intentionally," Tally explained.

"How was that received?"

"Not well, but I pointed out they could make the whole wedding about their dress mess or they could play it up like an asset." Theoretically, not all of the guests knew the sisters were perpetually at odds and would find it strange they wanted to match. Only their besties would know the truth, and only if they chose to tell them.

"Did the rest of the night go smoothly?" Mitch asked.

"For who? Not for me and Kayla, I assure you," she chuckled. "But the guests didn't know there were any problems, I don't think. The whole shindig was a little bit chaotic. I mean, hello, a wedding can be chaotic without having to do everything twice. Two rounds of toasts. Two first dances. Two daddy-daughter dances – the grooms shared a mother-son song, thank God."

Penelope and Pamela had insisted on putting their cakes as far apart as possible at the reception so the wedding planners had needed to herd the guests for the cake cutting twice. She got giggling again as she described herding drunk cats to her fiancé. Mitch appreciated the humor. He was a Georgia state trooper and he had a lot of experience moving inebriated groups around.

"I'm freaking exhausted. I hope I never get another double-wedding client again," Tally declared.

"You really mean that?" Mitch asked.

"No, of course not. Their budget was freaking ridiculous," Tally admitted. "I made a lot of money on this one. I can actually afford to pay myself after I've paid everybody else. But it seems like the bigger the budget, the whackier the wedding. I don't think that's my imagination."

"At least it wasn't a full moon this weekend." Weird things always happened during a full moon. Cops and wedding planners dreaded them.

"Seriously," she agreed. "To be fair, their father gave us a ginormous tip, and that makes tonight a little less painful. I split it three ways with Kayla and Yaya."

Tally pulled five crisp one hundred dollar bills out of her purse and put them on the sofa next to Mitch. "I figured we could use it to start our own wedding fund."

"Great idea."

"That should cover one tier of the cake," she joked. "If we have a small cake."

Mitch laughed. "We can go over all of that on the beach on Tuesday," he smiled. "I'm excited to help you choose some of the stuff. It's my wedding, too, ya know."

Tally patted her handsome husband-to-be on the hand and decided to tackle something that had been bothering her all day.

"Mitch, let's do our planning here at the house, and then go to the beach. I need my computer and a flat surface for writing. If a client wanted to plan on the beach, I'd say no because it's a big pain in the ass. We have everything we could possibly need up here."

"Does that mean we can't talk about our wedding on the beach?" he asked.

"We can. But I won't have exact prices or information on the beach. So it's nearly impossible to make actual decisions. Or take good notes."

"That makes sense," he agreed. "But can we get up in the morning to work on planning our wedding and still go to the beach in the afternoon?" He looked like a little kid negotiating with his parents.

"Sure. I don't think the planning is going to take me very long. This is what I do all day, every day. It's a question of how many opinions you have and what you want to have input on." Tally had every intention of letting Mitch choose some things for their wedding, but she was also ready to put the kibosh on anything tacky, overdone, or too expensive. "Have you started working on your guest list? We can't start planning if we have no idea how many guests we're going to have."

Tally had suggested Mitch get together with his mother and grandmother on their guest lists from the very beginning. The cost of a wedding for 50 guests was dramatically different from a wedding for 200 people. Tally's guest list wasn't that long, but everybody on it would come for sure. Mitch had more family in Glynn County than she had on her whole list. And that was after she added her Aunt Etah's list to hers.

"Um," Mitch hedged. "We've talked about the guest list a little bit."

"Have you actually written anything down?" Tally glared at him. "You've had months!"

"I'm sure mom and Bonnie have written down their lists. I figured I'd just look at theirs and add the people who are missing. Will mostly be my friends, I guess."

Tally was really mad at Mitch, but she was trying to control herself. She couldn't expect her state trooper fiancé to understand the financial nuances of wedding planning. But she had told him at least 10 times that she'd need the guest list before they could book anything.

"Okay, here's what we're going to do," she said with a smile usually reserved for clients who had not done their wedding planning homework. "Do you have to work tomorrow?"

Mitch was on assignment to a multi-state, multi-jurisdictional drug interdiction task force that was trying to stop the flow of drugs from Florida into Georgia. His hours depended on what they were investigating. He'd been shot in the head during a takedown the year before but, fortunately, the bullet hadn't hit anything important or done permanent damage. He'd survived. A hair one way or the other and he would've been dead, or at least a vegetable.

"I've got a stakeout tomorrow night, but I'm not busy during the day. Why?"

"You've got two days until my day off to get your list put together," she told him in a snippy tone. "If you don't, that's what we'll be doing on Tuesday afternoon instead of sitting on the beach. We can't start planning until we have the number of guests nailed down."

Mitch's face registered surprise, and Tally realized she was using her annoyed wedding planner voice on her future husband. It was after midnight and she'd just survived a double wedding with very difficult clients. It wasn't the right time to talk about their own wedding.

"I'm sorry. That sounded terrible," she admitted. "I didn't mean to talk to you like that. This is bad timing. I'm too fried to think."

She got up from the couch and stretched. She caught her reflection in the big glass windows that faced the ocean. Her curly blond hair had grown poofier from the humidity and her silhouette was distinctively that of a Troll doll.

"I'll be in a better mood after I've had a shower," she promised.

Mitch stood up and put his arms around Tally, then he kissed her firmly on the lips. "You're forgiven. But if you want to make it up to me, you could let me take a shower with you."

Tally groaned and headed into the master bedroom, with her fiancé hot on her heels.

Chapter 6

Mitch's mom texted Tally on Sunday morning and invited her to dinner at his parents' house that night. She said Mitch's older brother, Pete, and his wife, Robin, would be there, too. Roberta knew her youngest son, Mitch, probably had to work but she told her future daughter-in-law that she really wanted her to come anyway.

Mitch's mom and dad lived across the causeway in Brunswick. Tom Durham was on the Georgia State Patrol, too, and so were two of Mitch's three older brothers. Their grandfather had been in the first academy class of troopers sworn into the department after the state patrol was created by law in 1937. The brother Mitch was closest to in age, Pete, was a sergeant with the Glynn County Police Department. He'd taken a lot of good-spirited ribbing from his family for ignoring his third-generation law enforcement legacy on the GSP.

Roberta told Tally that Mitch had emailed her about the guest list in the middle of the night and she already had it in a spreadsheet for her.

"I can give you a printout tonight or just email it over to you," she texted. "It's got addresses and titles on it, so you should be good to go."

"Wow, that's great," Tally replied. She wasn't surprised that Mitch's mom was on top of things. She didn't have any daughters, and her soon-to-be daughter-in-law didn't have a mother. Aunt Etah wasn't in town most of the time so Roberta had already offered to go wedding gown shopping and cake tasting with her.

Tally's parents were killed in a plane crash when she was 12. Her father had been flying low along the north Florida coastline, in anticipation of wagging his wings at them on the front porch of Aunt Etah's oceanfront Jekyll Island home. The final investigation determined that he had suffered a heart attack and slumped over the yoke of the little plane, causing it to nose-dive into the ocean not far from Amelia Island. They were flying too low for her mother to prevent the crash and both of Tally's parents had died on impact when the plane hit the water.

After they were killed, Etah took Tally back home to her parents' historic rowhouse on Capitol Hill in DC, and they chose some favorite furniture and pictures to pack and move to Jekyll Island. The rowhouse was sold and the proceeds put into a significantly large trust fund. The trust paid for an all-girls' boarding school at St. Margaret's in Virginia and then Georgetown University for college.

Tally grew up in Etah's oceanfront beach house on Tallu Fish Lane. She spent all of her summers and school vacations on the smallest of Georgia's barrier islands. Jekyll Island, in its entirety, was a state park. It had a gate with an entrance fee on the causeway for visitors, and fewer than a thousand full-time residents.

Jekyll Island was originally a playground for very wealthy businessmen and their families (think the Astors, Morgans, and Pulitzers). They built the Jekyll Island Club, and then a series of private homes, along what's now known as "Millionaires Row," so they'd have a place to vacation and hunt when the weather up north became unpleasant. The state bought the island from the millionaires after World War II and declared it a state park for use by everyone.

The Jekyll Island Club Hotel was restored to its original glory and there were a number of chain hotels on the tiny island, too. In addition to overnight guests, thousands flocked to Jekyll to use its four golf courses, the clay-court tennis center, the soccer plex, and the waterpark operated by the Jekyll Island Authority. But even when the island was the most crowded, it still seemed empty to Tally, who'd spent her early Fourth of July celebrations on the National Mall in the nation's capital.

Tally's Aunt Etah and Mitch's grandmother, Bonnie, had been neighbors for longer than she'd been alive. They'd both been original owners of their homes on the northern end of the island. The front of Bonnie's house faced Beachview Drive and the backyard faced the back of Aunt Etah's house on Tallu Fish Lane. They had a huge family and they always included the Davis girls across the street in all of their celebrations and shenanigans. Tally had grown up feeling like a member of the Durham family.

Mitch and Tally were born the same summer and played together whenever Tally was on the island while they were growing up. Mitch's parents had bought a house on the mainland, across the water in Brunswick, so that Roberta wouldn't spend half her life on the causeway running the boys back and forth to Glynn Academy for school and football practice. Not that it had made much of a difference because everybody treated Bonnie's beach house like a command center during the warm months.

When Mitch got assigned to Post 35, the Georgia State Police barracks on Jekyll Island for a few months as a rookie, he'd moved into Bonnie's house. Shortly after that, Tally had evacuated from Vieques Island, Puerto Rico, where she'd been living and working for a wedding planner. The Category 5 storm had flattened anything that wasn't concrete on the little island seven miles off the coast of Puerto Rico.

She'd returned home to Jekyll to lick her wounds and figure out where to go next, but she ended up staying to launch her own wedding planning business on the tiny Georgia island where she'd grown up. Jekyll was known as the "gem of the Golden Isles" and had proven to be the perfect location for a wedding company, and later, a flower shop. She'd fallen in love with Mitch. And despite attempts to destroy her businesses by Mitch's crazy ex-girlfriend and a former client who couldn't take "no" for an answer, Tally's star continued to rise.

Yaya, her best friend from Vieques, moved to Jekyll to run the floral end of the wedding business for Tally. She wanted to expand the flower shop into an empty space next door and open a boutique, too. She pointed out that they had to have somebody in the flower shop all the time anyway during open hours. It wouldn't increase their staffing costs at all if they knocked a hole through the wall. They could always lock the doors and put up the closed signs if they needed to go all-hands-on-deck for a wedding.

"Maybe we should have just hired Brenda Fogel and saved everybody the grief," Tally joked.

Yaya rolled her eyes and gave Tally a look that said "don't even joke about that."

Her crazy former client had gone bonkers when Tally refused to give her a job on Jekyll. Brenda had business cards made up with Tally's logo and put Jekyll Weddings on her resume. Then she'd showed up at a big wedding dressed like Tally and pretended to be part of her staff. When all that failed to change Tally's mind, Brenda had tried to burn down the flower shop.

Fortunately for Tally, Brenda didn't know what she was doing and managed to set herself on fire instead of the shop. After a long recovery from her burns, she was awaiting trial in a maximum security state hospital in Milledgeville. Tally had no plans to visit her.

She knew Yaya was right about opening up a boutique, but Tally didn't feel like she could take on launching another business at the same time that she and Mitch were planning their wedding. She'd gently suggested to her fiancé that they plan on having a two-year engagement and knew from the look on Mitch's face that it wasn't an option. When she'd called Isabelle, her former boss from Vieques, to get advice, the older woman told her to hold off on expanding the business until she had her life together.

"And I don't mean when you can find the chair in your bedroom that's hiding under the pile clothes," Isabelle joked. "You're in love with a gorgeous and good man who loves you back. He wants to marry you. Do not put him off until the business doesn't need you so much because that time will never come."

Tally took her friend's advice to heart. Isabelle had spent years building up her company on Vieques only to lose it all overnight. They hadn't restored power to Vieques for 17 months after the storm, and the hospital on the little island was still condemned.

"I don't mean to be Debbie Downer, babe, but you never know what is going to happen. You're still on an island. You could get whacked tomorrow. Work isn't a glass ball," Isabelle said.

"A glass ball?"

"Haven't I told you this before? Maybe not," her mentor answered herself. "Okay, Tally – life is a series of balls that you have to juggle. Some of the balls are rubber and if you drop them, they bounce back. That's stuff like work, social activities, hobbies, etc. But some of the balls are glass – your health and your relationships are both glass, for example – and if you take your eye off either one of them, they could fall and be irreparably broken," she finished.

"So what are you saying?"

Isabelle sighed into the phone and Tally heard her. "I'm telling you that you can open a goddamned boutique whenever you want to, but you can't expect that hunky trooper to wait forever for you to make time for your own wedding. Do you guys fight a lot?"

"Not really. Not at all compared to Eduardo," Tally said.

"Ugh, don't compare Mitch to Eduardo. That's a total insult." Isabelle had never been a fan of Tally's boyfriend on Vieques. She'd warned her protégé to stay away from him too late and she'd watched Tally suffer through their tumultuous relationship.

"Okay, my point is that you can't take Mitch's love for granted," Isabelle continued. "It's great that he wants to get married and if you did anything else in the world for a living, you'd probably be going gangbusters with your own planning, torturing some innocent planner like yourself. But since this is what you do for a living, you're not as excited about it as a regular bride. You don't feel like a first-time bride."

"You may be right about that. He keeps trying to pin me down to discuss things and I don't think there's much to discuss. I know what works and what doesn't."

"But he doesn't," Isabelle continued. "You have to let him have the wedding planning experience. An abridged version of it at least."

"I am," Tally defended herself.

"Etah told me that Bonnie told her you said you didn't need to do a cake tasting because you'd already tasted every flavor of cake known to man that's available in Glynn County," Isabelle reported in a lecturing tone. "Now, is that really fair? And cake tasting is fun, why are you trying to avoid it?"

"I don't know. I guess I just feel dumb making vendors do all that work for something I already know the answer to."

"I get that, but I assure you that's not how Mitch feels. Sit down with your fiancé, pick a date, and do the planning. I promise you he'll lose interest after you sit down with him on it a couple of times," Isabelle said. "But you have to let him be a normal groom."

After she processed her conversation with Isabelle, Tally and Yaya had a long talk about the shop expansion and decided that they would start offering gift items for sale in the flower shop and see how that went. There was plenty of room to put shelves on the walls for displays. They could easily replace the existing counter with a cabinet that contained a glass display for jewelry and other more expensive items. If it was successful, they could expand the space the next year. If somebody else rented next door from the Jekyll Island Authority in the meantime, then it wasn't meant to be.

Chapter 7

"How was it?" Cheryl asked when she picked up Tally's phone call that night.

Tally had called her friend on the way to dinner with Mitch's family and promised a follow-up from the car on the way home. "It was pretty good, actually. At least now I know how many they have on the guest list."

Cheryl chuckled. She ran weddings on Sea Island at The Cloister, one of the poshest venues on the coast of Georgia. And, like all wedding planners, she knew the planning couldn't start until there was an approximate headcount. There was no way to know what the bride and groom could afford to do unless the planner knew how many people she needed to keep fed, watered, and entertained. And that rule held true even if the planner was also the bride.

"I only have about 30 people on my list – and that's including you and Etah and Yaya and Kayla," Tally laughed. "But Roberta had about 100 on her 'initial list,' as she called it. Bonnie has a list, too. But Roberta said it's a lot of overlap so not to freak out. I noticed there are a couple of duplicates from my list, too. So, I can cross them off her list. If Mitch wants to invite a lot of his police friends, we're going to hit 200."

"So, how is that plan to have a small wedding going?" Cheryl joked.

"It's out the window, I guess. Dang," she grumped. "That's a lot of people."

"Yeah, but if you do it at the Jekyll Club Hotel, you'll get your member discount plus you know Mayra will hook you up all over the place with deals. You send her so much business on a daily basis."

"Mayra's on my guest list, too," Tally moaned. Cheryl started laughing.

"Look, a lot of your friends are in the event industry and we expect to help on your wedding day. That's just how it goes. If I ever find a victim, I'm making you plan my wedding for free," she announced.

It had the desired effect and Tally giggled. "I'd be honored. I'd let you plan mine except I can't afford anything on Sea Island."

"True that. But your heart is on Jekyll anyway. You shouldn't get married anywhere else. I've planned a few weddings on Jekyll myself so if you need help..." she joked. Cheryl had been the in-house wedding planner at Jekyll Island Club Hotel for several years before a management change made her lose her mind and quit.

"Are you allowed back in the hotel?" Tally laughed. Cheryl had given all of the pending brides the general manager's cell phone number when she quit, and she'd been persona non grata on the property for a while after that.

"Shut up, you know I am. I was never completely banned since my family are still members. I just had to avoid the management, until he got fired," she laughed.

"That's good, because I want you to be a bridesmaid," Tally said.

"Oh Tally, thank you. I'd love to. Are you going to make us all wear ugly dresses so that you look better?" she teased.

"You know it," Tally retorted. "I'm going to use every evil tactic I've ever learned from a bride so we can have a miserable wedding weekend."

"Sounds fab. Wouldn't miss it."

"You'd better not. Who better to bustle my dress? You've already seen me naked." Both women laughed.

Every wedding planner had spent too much time on her knees under brides' dresses bustling them and, frequently, having to McGyver broken bustles with diaper pins after careless guests stepped on the back of the gown and the ribbons that held it all together ripped. They got quite the view over the years as most brides opted to go commando under their dresses to make using the bathroom easier.

"Well, you've gotta be feeling a lot better about things now that you have the numbers. Don't forget to let Mitch have some input when you guys sit down to plan," Cheryl reminded her.

"Have you been talking to Isabelle?"

"No. Why?"

"Huh," Tally grunted, not believing her entirely. "Don't worry – I'm going to let him choose a few things. Like the groom's cake."

"You're going to have a groom's cake?" Cheryl sounded surprised. Grooms' cakes were exclusively a southern thing before the famous bleeding armadillo groom's cake in the movie "Steel Magnolias."

"I don't know," Tally laughed. "Only if he wants one. And if he does, it'll probably have a cop theme. Maybe I can convince him to save the money and put a blue ribbon around the bottom tier of the wedding cake?"

"Oh Tally," Cheryl groaned. "I'm glad I'm not Mitch."

"Really?"

"A little bit," her friend answered honestly. "Try to remember that this is supposed to be fun for him even if it's just an extension of work for you."

"Fair enough. I'll keep that in mind." Tally saw a repeating theme in the advice her friends were giving her. Maybe she should start taking it.

Chapter 8

Everything Mitch and Tally had discussed about not planning on the beach became moot when they woke up to gray sky and drizzle on Tuesday. Tally forced herself to get out of their cozy bed and post a blog to her web page, and she was on her third cup of coffee by the time her fiancé emerged, sleep rumpled, from the bedroom.

"Good morning, sunshine!" she greeted him in an annoyingly perky voice.

"Who said it was 'good'?" Mitch joked as he popped a pod into the Nespresso machine that Etah had kindly left with them when she moved into her new condo.

Her aunt had gifted them her oceanfront home as a wedding gift at their engagement party, and she'd moved her personal belongings out as soon as the newly-built home she referred to as "her penthouse" was ready for occupancy. She hadn't taken much of the furniture with her to the new condo in The Moorings next to the marina. Etah claimed she'd always wanted to hire an interior designer and start from scratch, but Tally suspected her aunt didn't want to leave them in an empty house they needed to furnish.

It had worked out well for the engaged couple. Tally loved the beach house just as it was, and only planned to change things as stuff wore out and needed to be replaced. Nine months of the year, they spent the bulk of their free time outside on the deck overlooking the water, anyway. The kitchen had been redone a few years earlier and wouldn't need a facelift for a long time. The only thing she and Mitch had talked about changing, way down the road, was the actual size of the house. It was technically only one story, although it had a cinderblock garage beneath it that they used for storage. They were allowed to go up another level, or they could rethink how they were using the "basement" level. There were no actual basements on Jekyll because of the water table being so high. Twice that Tally remembered, storm waters had breached the dunes and the garage had been flooded. It didn't matter because Aunt Etah kept everything in there up on shelves, but they couldn't use that level for anything else unless they figured out how to waterproof it first. Mitch had bet that would be more expensive than building up another level.

"We're not going to the beach today, are we?" Mitch asked once he'd sipped enough of his coffee to think clearly.

"Doesn't look like it. That means we'll be able to get lots done here instead," she told him enthusiastically.

"Great," Mitch said, but his tone conveyed anything but excitement. He was not a morning person regardless of the time of day.

When Mitch moved in, after Etah moved out, Tally transferred her clothing and accessories into the master bedroom they were going to share, and they'd stored all of Mitch's arriving boxes in her old bedroom so he could go through them one at a time. They weren't packed in any rational order because he'd moved so many times in the past couple of years. Tally suspect Roberta had taken advantage of the opportunity to clean out her own attic and garage because several boxes she'd peeked into held memorabilia from his childhood, including sports trophies, report cards, and yearbooks.

Tally's plan was to keep her wardrobe and Mitch's everyday clothes in the closet and dressers in the master bedroom that had been her aunt's room. Etah had installed a good closet system and there was enough space for them both. Tally's old bedroom would become Mitch's man cave, although Tally would keep her file cabinets and printers in there, too. She was going to order a closet system from The Container Store that would hold everything he'd brought with him. She couldn't believe how many kinds of police uniforms he had, or how much gear he needed to store. He had an everyday ballistic vest, another bigger vest he'd been issued when he joined the task force, different inserts for the vests, and a helmet and giant bullet-proof shield (she didn't know what that was for and probably didn't want to). He also needed a whole charging station for phones, radios, flashlights, night vision goggles, and some other police gadgets she couldn't name. He'd ordered a big gun safe from Tractor Supply that would fit in one corner and it was due to be delivered at the end of the week, so Tally had to force him to tackle the mess or at least cut a path through it.

Mitch worried that Tally would be sad to see her bedroom turned into what he had started calling "The Armory," but she was really okay with it. She'd grown up there and had all the good memories. She wanted Mitch to feel like it was his house now, too. Giving him a space that wasn't pink would help, she thought as she picked up the paint samples that had been sitting on the counter for a week.

"Did you look at these?" she asked.

"Yeah, they all look the same to me. You pick something," he told her, not looking up from the copy of the Brunswick News he was reading.

One of the paint chips was shades of blue, another had shades of cream and sand, the third was a variety of different grays. Nothing alike. Tally picked up the sand one she favored and dropped the rest in the trash.

"Okay, that's settled. We need to pick up paint and get that room ready before your new gun safe is delivered. We have three days," she reminded him.

"Why are we trying to paint it and unpack at the same time?"

"Because once they put that 1,500-pound monstrosity of a safe in the room, we'll not be able to move it to paint behind it. And it'll look like crap from the side if you can see pink." Tally knew she sounded less nice than she should, but they'd already had this conversation. She hated it when Mitch acted like a bride who didn't like the word "no" so pretended he didn't hear it.

"I thought we were wedding planning today, not unpacking me," Mitch grumped as he folded up the paper and set it aside. "It's bad enough that we can't go to the beach."

He sounded like a little kid and it made Tally laugh.

"We'll still do the wedding planning stuff today," she promised. "In fact, why don't we tackle that first and get it over with?"

"Get it over with?" he sounded genuinely disappointed. "I thought it was something fun to do."

Tally remembered what Isabelle and Cheryl had said to her about her attitude and tried to adjust it.

"It is fun. I just said 'get it over with' in the context of let's get that part done before we have to suffer through dealing with that room," she tried to save herself.

"Uh huh," Mitch said. "Sure, that's what you meant." He stood up from the table and put his coffee cup in the kitchen sink. "I'm going to go take a shower and then I'm at your disposal. But this is supposed to be a fun day off, so let's not do only work stuff. Okay?"

He crossed the kitchen and kissed her. "Okay," she agreed, feeling that flutter she still got when Mitch was romantic.

"Can we plan our wedding naked?" he asked, reaching to squeeze her butt.

"No," she laughed and stepped away. "Go shower."

"Why?" he whined.

"Because we'd never get anything accomplished today if we started out like that."

"Fine, but you owe me a playday," he said.

Chapter 9

The wedding planning session had been hilarious, and Tally regretted not having started the process sooner. Mitch made outrageous suggestions – having a live alligator at the reception, for example - and then she gave him a reality check and then they'd compromised on something they could both live with. Pretty much every time.

There were a few things that she'd let him win on that she wasn't actually going to let stand – for example, they were not going to decorate their entire reception in a Thin Blue Line theme, regardless of the stuff Mitch had found on Pinterest. But it made Tally laugh when she looked at his board, and the fact that he'd cared enough sign up for a Pinterest account said a lot.

Isabelle had taught her wedding planners that it was important to listen to the groom's opinions, because they usually didn't have many and she believed they should be able to have some of the things they wanted because it was their big day, too. Tally planned to work the blue line elements into the welcome party or the rehearsal dinner or some other aspect of their wedding weekend. Maybe they'd put something in the welcome bags for the out-of-town guests, too. But she was not willing to have people see her wedding photos and wonder if she got married at the Policeman's Ball. The ribbon on the cake might not be a bad idea either, now that she thought about it seriously.

Mitch had made his guest list and, once Tally removed duplications from his mother's and grandmother's lists, the headcount wasn't as bad as she'd thought. About 150 guests, in total, between the two of them. So that was their number to work with when deciding what they wanted to do and how much they wanted to spend.

Tally and Mitch went through her normal client checklist together, line-by-line, discussing who would marry them (the state police chaplain who his family had known forever), whether they wanted to write their own vows (they did not), and if they wanted to hire a babysitter to be on site to deal with the little kids (yes, absolutely).

Some of the questions they could answer easily, some required additional research – like what kind of deal the local bands Tally worked with all the time might give them for their own events – and some things they needed to think about, like whether to have a farewell brunch the day after their own wedding even though they both hated attending them as guests.

They both got laughing hysterically after Mitch pointed out that Tally explained almost every element by saying, "Well, most of my clients do such-and-such, but that's not how we want to go about it." It was true.

When they'd accomplished all they could without Tally getting out her computer, she suggested they move on to dealing with her old bedroom. Mitch couldn't talk her out of it.

They had already moved her bed from the room before Mitch's boxes were brought in, and only a dresser, desk, and mostly-empty bookshelf remained. The plan was to install a Murphy bed so the space could also be a guestroom.

Tally suggested that one of them should run pick up the paint while the other one pulled everything out of the room and starting taping.

"I thought we were spending today together," Mitch complained.

"This is my only day off. If I don't help you get this finished today, it's up to you to recruit your brother to help you. Otherwise, you're going to be stuck with a pink gun room," she warned.

"Okay fine. You go get the paint while I move the boxes. You can't lift some of them."

Tally gave him a look but didn't argue. She was getting what she wanted.

"I'm going to call my buddy at Home Depot's paint desk and he'll probably have it ready for me when I get there. There's a tub in the garage labeled 'Painting Supplies' and it has everything we're going to need in it," she told him. "Would you be a doll and bring that up? It's got painter's tape in it too, so if you get the room emptied out, you could start taping off the edges.

"Maybe we should paint the ceiling, too, while we're at it," she suggested, looking up.

Mitch gave her a look, then peered at the ceiling before focusing on Tally again. "It doesn't really need it."

"Okay, your call. It's your room," she told him as she padded to their bedroom to get ready to leave. What she was really thinking in her head was that the ceiling in there was going to look terrible after they painted the ceiling in the hallway that abutted it. Because that was also on her to-do list, she just hadn't mentioned it to Mitch yet.

Chapter 10

When Tally got back from Home Depot about 90 minutes later, Mitch was talking on his phone and pacing. She stayed out of his way but made no effort to give him privacy because she wanted to know what was going on. Mitch caught her staring and winked at her.

"Okay, I'll see you in about an hour. That's fine. Yeah, I got it. Nope, all good. Bye." He hung up and kissed his fiancée. "I have to go into work."

"I figured." She wasn't annoyed. She loved that Mitch loved his job as much as she loved hers. It made it a lot easier for both of them to deal with the times when they couldn't be together because of work. Mitch's dad, Tom, swore he hadn't had a holiday off from work the first 10 years he was a trooper. Mitch had a little more flexibility since he wasn't on patrol. But working for the task force, he got paged a lot. "Anything interesting?"

"I think so. Joe didn't tell me that much. Just said he'd gotten a call and they'd told him to call me in, too. And to dress in casual plain clothes with vests on underneath, but bring the rumble gear. So I think we're doing something, I just don't know what."

He sounded excited and Tally tried not to let the fear she felt in her gut show on her own face. It had only been a year since she'd sat at his bedside praying the bullet that struck his head hadn't done any perma-nent damage.

"Okay, well be careful out there. And touch base with me once you know what you're up to or I'll be up worrying all night." She wasn't kidding. She'd learned that some cop wives, including her future sis-ter-in-law, Robin, listened to their husband's department's radio chat-ter on a scanner when they were working. Tally couldn't do that even if she wanted to, since Mitch was detailed to a task force. It was probably for the best.

Mitch went to dress and Tally checked out the progress he'd made in her old bedroom. It was as empty as it needed to be and he'd taped off the woodwork around the windows. She got on the ladder to finish what he had started. No reason she couldn't get the first coat of paint up on the ceiling and the walls herself. She'd call Yaya and Cheryl to try to bribe them to help.

"I'm sorry I have to leave," Mitch told Tally in a voice that said he meant it and kissed her goodbye. She was just about his height standing on the second step of the ladder.

"I know. Go! I'm going to call in some reinforcements and see how much I can still get done without you," she said. "Stay safe and check in with me when you can."

"I will," he promised and kissed her again before he left.

When she finished the taping, Tally took a break. She made coffee while she called Yaya on speaker to beg her to help paint.

"I would, but I have a date," her friend explained.

"What?" Tally was delighted. "With who? How do I not know about this?"

Yaya giggled. "I just met him this morning. At the coffee shop near my house. Turns out, we're neighbors."

"And how old is he? What does he do for a living? Is he hot? Is he Puerto Rican?"

"He's not Boricua," Yaya said, using a slang term for the Puerto Rican people. "But he's Catholic, so my mom would like him."

Tally laughed. "But seriously, what does he do?"

"You won't even believe it. He's a deputy with the Glynn County Sheriff's Office. And yes, he knows the Durhams," she answered the question as Tally was thinking it. "His name is Matt Baker, and he's 30, and he's hot. He's black with light greenish hazel eyes. His hair is super short, but it looks good on him."

"Tell me more. I'm loving this."

"I just bet you are," Yaya said. "You're nosy."

"No I'm not. I just care," Tally told her with an innocent tone, and then laughed.

"He's from Jacksonville originally. Went to Howard University in DC for college and then went straight into law enforcement in Glynn County. He started out working at the jail but now he mostly serves warrants and transports prisoners to court or doctor's appointments."

"So what are you guys doing tonight?" Tally asked, intrigued. Yaya was super picky and hadn't had a lot of boyfriends because few men met her standards.

"He's taking me to dinner at a crab place. Not sure which one."

"Oof," Tally said with sympathy. "What are you wearing?"

"Right?" Yaya ranted. "None of my first-date worthy tops are things that I want to drip crab guts and butter all over. But nothing I'd usually wear to eat crabs is flattering."

"You know what you have to do, right?"

"What?"

"Make the sacrifice, Yaya," Tally said in a serious tone. "Which shirt is the hot deputy worthy of destroying tonight?"

"Fine! Alright. It's the purple off the shoulder top with the smocking at the waist."

"Oh, that's a cute one. Sure you're willing to ruin it?" Tally asked.

"Dammit Tally. Now I'm not. Maybe I should wear the yellow one with the flowers? I could potentially be able to save that one with enough Spray and Wash."

"You know what, Yaya? As excited as you sound, I say go with the purple. But make it worth it."

"I plan to," her friend agreed.

Tally called Cheryl next but only got voicemail. Her friend was probably running some event at The Cloister.

She went back into The Armory – she was trying to remember to call it that in her head – and took it all in. She spread the drop cloths that Mitch had pulled out of her painting tub on the floor around the perimeter of the room and then added another in the center for good measure. Tally always made a mess when she painted. Then she opened up the bucket of ceiling paint and got started with a goal of finishing the whole room before Mitch got home. It would be a fun surprise.

Chapter 11

Mitch was gone for two days. He'd called Tally to explain late Tuesday night and warned he might not be able to break away from his assignment for a few days. He promised to touch base daily, but he also told her not to worry if she texted him and he didn't reply immediately. He was working undercover and wouldn't always have his personal phone on him. He said he couldn't tell her much more about it on the phone. Tally's stomach dropped at the news but she sucked it up and made sure her dismay didn't show in her voice. Mitch sounded really excited.

"Well, have fun and be safe. Be super safe. Be really, really careful," she told him.

"I will. I promise," he'd said.

True to his word, he checked in frequently for the next few days, although he didn't tell her what he was up to.

Tally went about life as usual because that was what she was supposed to do, according to Robin. She said that she'd never get anything done if she stopped what she was doing every time her police sergeant husband jumped into his police car and hit the sirens as he left the driveway. As a police official who lived in the community he served, Pete frequently had to go into work when he was supposed to be off. He got called if something major happened or one of his officers screwed up. Tally had weddings to plan, flowers to order, and a business to run even when Mitch was working undercover, and she did her very best to take advantage of the alone time to get focused.

On Wednesday night, Yaya and Kayla had come home from the flower shop with Tally to help finish painting Mitch's room. She called Red Bug Pizza and ordered two large specials, thinking leftover cold pizza would make an awesome breakfast. Yaya made her famous deadly mojitos and kept the other women's cups full while they painted and by the time they left, the room was painted and the floors swept clean of debris. Tally decided she needed to go buy a rug for the room before the giant safe arrived. It hadn't needed it when most of the floor space was her bed, but it felt a little cold with the bare tile floor once the big furniture was gone.

She worked from her dining room table part of Thursday and then went into the flower shop to get a few things done before a meeting with a potential client. She'd invited Kayla to tag along and was pleased to find the young wedding planner had worn a cute sleeveless dress with a matching jacket. Tally hoped that, eventually, Kayla would be able to handle pitching new brides and grooms on her own. She could already plan and execute all but the worst weddings by herself. Now she needed to learn how Tally brought in the clients. Marketing was a time suck, and she didn't usually pull her staff from the office for potential client meetings because she didn't need to have them there. Tally had about a 75 percent success rate at booking brides and grooms who actually came to meet with her in person before signing a contract. But she wasn't entirely sure how to explain her methods to Kayla. Tally was hoping the younger girl would pick it up through observation or osmosis if she attended enough meet-and-greets with couples who ended up hiring Jekyll Weddings.

Unfortunately, that consultation turned out to be a dud. Tally and Kayla met the brides on the pool deck of the Jekyll Ocean Club, the ocean side of the Jekyll Island Club Resort. After introductions, Tally led the women on a tour of the property and talked about options for using it. They'd met there because Sophia Summers, the bride who'd reached out to Tally, had specifically asked if she planned weddings at that particular venue. Tally resisted the urge to tell her to go look at the website and assured the bride that she had an excellent relationship with the hotel on both sides of its property.

Sophia's fiancée, Eliza Huntington, wanted something "modern and fresh" for their wedding weekend, which meant Tally wouldn't bother to mention the beautiful historic wedding sites available. The Westin was already booked on their first-choice wedding date with another one of Tally's brides, although they hadn't told Sophia and Eliza that. Tally just said it was unavailable.

In order to expand her business, she had to start splitting up from Kayla so they could run separate sets of events on the same days. They'd done it a few times but Tally kept finding herself running back and forth between clients to troubleshoot. That could have been because Kayla drew some real nutjobs for her client list, or it might have been Tally overreacting and not giving her protégé a chance to triage things herself. But she had to get to a point where they could have multiple huge groups on the island at one time if Tally wanted to be able to see any real growth in her business.

The brides they were meeting with looked like professional women – they were both wearing pastel suits and heels (Sophia wore a skirt and Eliza had a pantsuit) and their makeup was perfect. Sophia was blonde and Eliza was brunette, but other than that, nothing stood out as different about them. It was a little weird. Tally had a moment of deju vu and realized she was suffering a little PTSD from the Beauregard sisters. She made a mental note to mention it to Kayla later.

Sophia and Eliza seemed like easy brides during the tour of property, but when they sat down to talk details and dollars, things took a quick turn. Tally told the couple how much the wedding they were talking about hosting – 250-plus guests for four days of events with top-shelf bars and live music – was going to cost and Eliza flipped her lid.

"That's ridiculous. How much is your mark-up on services?" she demanded of Tally and Kayla.

"We don't mark up outside vendor services," Tally explained. "You pay us a percentage of your overall wedding budget, but the numbers you're agreeing to and signing contracts for are the real thing.

"You pay us half of our fee up front when you sign the contract, and you'll be writing checks and making credit card payments directly to your vendors and venues from that point on," she continued. "The money doesn't go through my company's bank account. Our fee is based on the final budget and the second half of that is due, based on the final, actual cost of the wedding, 30 days prior to your wedding date, along with all of your balances due to your vendors."

It was a pretty straightforward way of doing things and it kept Tally's tax paperwork simple. Few clients had a problem with it.

"I don't like that," Sophia said after Tally finished.

I don't care what you think, Tally thought but didn't say. She looked at Kayla and could tell the younger girl was thinking the same thing.

"That's how it works, and we do it the same way for all of our clients," she explained.

"And you're the only wedding planner on Jekyll Island?" Eliza asked as she pulled out a cigarette.

"I'm sorry, you can't smoke that in here," Tally told her. Smoking inside was pretty much illegal everywhere and she wondered what the bride was thinking.

"Figures," Eliza grumped and put the cigarette pack back into her Coach purse.

"I'm the only wedding planner who lives on Jekyll right now, but there are other wedding planners in the area that plan weddings on this island." She didn't want these women as clients anyway. There was no point in wasting her breath explaining why it was better to work with somebody who was based where the wedding was held.

"What about on my wedding day? If we book the whole place, I want to be able to smoke," Eliza had a one-track mind.

"I'd imagine that we can make arrangements to have ashtrays available in outside spots around the venue, but you're not going to be allowed to smoke inside," Tally explained in a polite, but no-nonsense, voice. "If that's what you want, we should look into private houses or villas where the owners might consent to you smoking inside for a hefty extra fee. But none of the hotels on Jekyll are going to allow it."

While Eliza was asking questions, Sophia had been running numbers on the pad of paper inside a Gucci portfolio she'd pulled out of her Chanel purse.

"Are we looking at over $100,000?" she suddenly asked.

"It doesn't have to be. The cost, per person, for your events is based on the choices that you make. If you want to have an open, top-shelf bar at all of your events..."

"We do," Eliza interrupted.

"And you want four days of events for 250 people. And live music at your events and a big band at your wedding with a DJ to play during breaks. You talked about wanting to go down the aisle under a flower arch. How big of an arch? What kind of flowers? Orchids are much more expensive than carnations, for example."

When neither woman said anything, Tally continued. "Tell me what your end goal budget is and I'll tell you if it's doable, or rather, what you have to do in order to spend that amount of money. There are lots of options here. Do fewer events. Do less expensive things for your welcome party. Don't have huge wedding parties. Or do absolutely everything you want and invite fewer guests. It's all up to you."

"I don't want to spend a penny over $50,000," Sophia declared.

"I thought we said $75,000," Eliza snapped at her fiancée.

"*You* said 75," Sophia hissed back.

The women sat glaring at each other as if Tally and Kayla weren't even there. The standoff went on for more than a minute.

"Alrighty," Tally finally said. She'd had enough. "It has been lovely meeting you ladies. But it sounds like you still have some thinking to do about what you want to spend. Please let me know if you have any questions." She began to put her notepad into her purse.

"That's it?" Sophia asked.

"What else would you like to do or see while you're here? If you only want a modern venue, this is your option for that wedding date. If you're willing to move the date, we can go look at The Westin. Jekyll is known for being a historic state park and most of the venues capitalize on history of the island so you don't have a bunch of modern options. There are places on St. Simons worth exploring if you're interested in going wider with your venue search," Tally suggested, hoping they'd say no. "But if you want to get married here, at this venue, you need to have a realistic budget for what you want before we can work together."

"We'll discuss it," Eliza said and stood up. Tally and Kayla stood up, too, and said their goodbyes. Only Sophia looked disappointed the consultation was finished.

As they walked toward the exit of Jekyll Ocean Club, Tally made eye contact with her friend Olivia, a member of senior management, and made a face. The subtle message would let Olivia know that the women she'd met with were unlikely to be her clients. If Olivia wanted to give it a shot and convince them to book their wedding at the property, she could have a go at it. But Tally was out unless they came back to her waving a big fat budget. She didn't book contracts with unrealistic numbers.

Chapter 12

Kayla would welcome the bride and groom who were arriving for their Saturday wedding later that afternoon without any help from her boss, which was exactly how things were supposed to be in Tally's master plan.

"You look fabulous so just go dressed as you are," Tally suggested. "Do you need my help with anything?"

The wedding of Alita Davani and Juan Velasquez was going to be an unusual one. The bride's family was from Iran – "Persia" her father corrected them on the first planning conference call – but she had lived in the United States her whole life. Her boyfriend, Juan, was from San Juan, Puerto Rico, and had moved north after Hurricane Maria, just like Tally. He got a job working in Alita's father's auto body shop in the Atlanta suburbs and, before long, found himself engaged to his boss's youngest daughter.

The family was doing most of the wedding work themselves. They'd hired Jekyll Weddings to help them find a venue that would allow what they wanted, and to plan all the aspects of the wedding except the food. Alita's family would be cooking everything and serving a "traditional Persian wedding feast."

Juan's family had traveled from Puerto Rico to attend the wedding and, as a nod to them, there would be two wedding ceremonies. One a traditional Christian ceremony and the other a traditional Persian ceremony. While Tally was excited to plan a Persian wedding (she was always thinking about the marketing photos she'd get out of something different), she did not get excited when she learned their ceremony would involve live birds. Doves, specifically. There was a point at the end of their traditional ceremony where the birds would be released by the bride and groom. Tally's previous experiences with having live animals at weddings – horses, dogs, cats, ferrets, and a pet iguana, once – had never been particularly good. They all made messes that nobody dressed for a wedding wanted to clean up.

Kayla had gotten permission from the venue for the birds, with a hefty cleaning deposit. And the doves had to stay outside on the porch. They weren't allowed inside the rental house. Tally told Kayla to make sure she let the clients know - on no uncertain terms - that they were responsible for dealing with the birds and their mess. The wedding planning team would not be handling the birds or dealing with them in any way. Tally told Kayla to blame their insurance if the father of the bride balked at the restrictions. But the parents of the bride were fine with that plan and assured Kayla they would handle absolutely everything related to the wedding reception food and the damned birds.

Alita and Juan weren't having an official welcome party or any other pre-wedding events that Jekyll Weddings needed to execute. Just the Christian ceremony on the beach, followed by the Persian ceremony in the yard of the villa. The women in Alita's family would prepare all the reception food and Jekyll Weddings would provide some décor, the DJ, and have caterers set up a limited bar on the pool deck for five hours. The clients had opted to bring plastic silverware and plates, and paper napkins – all in pink – so Tally told Kayla not to bother to get pictures of their dinner tables for the file.

Kayla planned to check in with Alita and Juan when they arrived and see if any last-minute problems had popped up. She wouldn't see them again until the wedding on Saturday unless they needed something. They weren't doing a ceremony setup on the beach – everyone was standing – so all Kayla had to do earlier in the day was deliver the bouquets to the bridal party. The mother-of-the-bride had made all the centerpieces at home out of silk flowers and was bringing them to Jekyll Island. Tally took issue with fake flowers at an outside wedding surrounded by real flowers, but she wasn't the bride, so she'd kept her opinions to herself. It was along the same lines as how she felt about them using paper and plastic at an actual wedding reception.

Yaya was processing the flowers for the Davani/Velasquez wedding when Tally and Kayla got back to the shop. She was also processing a lot more flowers for two other weddings on the island that weekend that hadn't used Jekyll Weddings for planning. Tally loved that. They cleared a bigger profit on flowers than weddings, to be perfectly honest. She gave her own brides and grooms a 20-percent discount on their flowers. If Tally didn't love planning the weddings so much, she'd focus entirely on the floral end of the industry and make a lot more money. But as it was, she had the best of both worlds.

"You need any help?" Tally asked her best friend.

Yaya was a whizz at taking the flowers that arrived from their boxes and prepping them. Most blooms had to be carefully removed from netting or plastic. Lots of heat-sensitive flowers arrived with water tubes on their stems. She freed all of it and trimmed the stems on an angle before putting them in big buckets of water with preservative that would fit into the bottom of their floral fridge. She was much faster than Tally.

"Nah, I'm almost done," Yaya waved her off. "If you're going to be around tomorrow, we have about 300 roses to murder for brides' aisles and you know I hate the way they scream when I depetal them."

Tally laughed. Yaya made the most horrendous noises when she was "murdering" roses so Tally did it when she had time. It was sort of therapeutic if they weren't in a big rush.

"I'll plan to do that," Tally volunteered. "If you don't need me for anything else, I'm going to go finish assembling Mitch's room. I'm hoping the blinds and rug I ordered from Amazon have arrived. I'd love to have them in before he gets home tomorrow."

"He'll be home tomorrow?"

"That's what his text earlier today said. But he said he'd confirm with me in the morning so I'm not making any hot plans for us this weekend," she laughed. "The ginormous gun safe he ordered for that room is being delivered in the morning and I have to be ready for it. Once it's there, it's never moving ever again."

Chapter 13

Tally didn't realize how true that was until the safe arrived at the house. Mitch's older brother, Pete, had come over to help her with the installation and to figure out why the blinds she'd purchased weren't fitting her windows correctly. The whole process was much easier than Tally had anticipated, and the safe did not drop through the floor when the deliverymen took it off the dolly, as she had feared. The house was almost 50 years old and she'd been worried. The big box took up a quarter of the floor space in the room.

Mitch had insisted on buying a waterproof, fireproof safe that would have enough room to hold all of his personal and work guns, Tally's good jewelry, and their more important paper documents.

"This house is waterfront, Tally. We need to take every precaution to protect things in case the island gets hit by a big storm," he said more than once.

She was glad his brother had come over before the safe arrived. Pete had known to leave some space around the safe for cleaning, and he'd also fixed the blinds – turned out, she had put something in backwards on the mounts. Before he left, Pete helped her hang some display shelves on the walls to surprise Mitch. Tally had found boxes of police cars and fire trucks that her fiancé collected over the years in the pile and decided they'd look cool displayed on the walls of The Armory. If Mitch didn't like how she'd decorated the room for him, he could switch it up. But for now, she thought it looked pretty good. At least it got rid of the boxes.

After Pete left, Tally sat on the floor of Mitch's new room with a pack of Windex wipes and washed all of the police cars, firetrucks, and other random first responder vehicles she'd found. She didn't know if they'd ever lived anywhere but in a box, but she wasn't going to show off dirty vehicles. Even if that was probably closer to how they looked in real life, she amused herself thinking as she worked.

There was a huge picture window in the room, and two smaller windows. She'd gotten the blinds for the small windows, and when the shelves on the wall were finished, she opened the package with the new curtains she'd ordered for the big picture window. They were black with a blue line for law enforcement across the middle. She hated the way they looked. But she knew Mitch would love it, so she had also purchased a heavy ivory curtain to hang behind it, facing out. The curtains would be drawn almost all of the time because of the gun safe and she didn't want to pull into her driveway and see the blue line curtain. It was cute on the inside but didn't have the curb appeal she wanted on their beach house. Flying a Thin Blue Line flag beneath the American flag on the front porch would have to suffice.

She and Etah had gone to an attorney's office after the engagement party so her aunt could officially change the home's ownership to Tallulah Davis, Tally's legal name. It was a little trickier than transferring the average house because all of the property on Jekyll was owned by the state park and managed by the Jekyll Island Authority. Homeowners had long-term land-lease agreements with the state that protected their investment. The woman who managed the leases for the authority helped them finish the paperwork. Etah reminded Tally to send Kathy Marks flowers as a thank you for her assistance.

Etah had announced she was giving Mitch and Tally her house at their engagement party, but it was actually their wedding gift. She'd already bought her new condo in the marina by the Jekyll bridge, and there was no reason for them to wait to start building their lives together. However, she'd only put Tally's name on the house at first. She advised her great-niece that she could add Mitch's name to the house after they were legally married. But Etah didn't believe in owning property together before marriage. Mitch agreed with her and had no problem with the plan.

Her aunt had given them a really sweet sign as a housewarming present. It read "Mitch & Tally's Island Home, Est. 2019." Tally hung it inside their front door to surprise her fiancé and had just finished putting the step stool and hammer away when he arrived.

"Lucy, I'm home," Mitch bellowed in his best Ricky Ricardo voice.

Tally ran to the front door to greet him. He swept her up in a hug that became a long, deep kiss.

"I missed you," he said when he stopped to take a breath.

"I missed you more." They both chuckled.

Mitch went out to his truck to haul in the rest of his gear, and Tally dragged the first duffle he'd brought in over to the washing machine. She'd just unzipped it when he warned her not to mix her clothes with his.

"Some of that stuff is seriously nasty. Mud, sweat, and spit, among other things," he explained.

"Ew. Okay, I'll leave it for you to do." *Not my department,* she thought and wrinkled her nose.

"Probably smart," he agreed.

"I have a big surprise for you," she announced.

"Did the safe arrive?" Mitch sounded excited. "I'm sorry you had to handle that. I'm assuming it didn't fall through the floor or you would have called?"

"Oh shut up," Tally laughed. "Go look at 'The Armory' and see if you like what I've done with it. It's your room but I didn't want to leave everything on the floor, so you might want to rearrange things..." Mitch was already headed down the hall to her old bedroom.

He stopped in the doorway.

"Holy moly, this is awesome!" he blurted, then went into the room for a closer examination. "I love the cars on the walls – that was such a cool idea!"

"Yeah, well I washed each itty bitty windshield on every car, truck, and train but you're in charge of vehicle maintenance from now on," she joked.

"This is really awesome, Tally. Thank you so much for doing all of this."

She smiled and stood on tip toes to help her reach his lips for a kiss. "I'm glad you like it."

Her phone rang down the hall and disrupted their canoodling.

"That's Isabelle's ring tone."

"Go answer it," Mitch told her. "I need a shower before you get any closer to me. Then I want to take you out to dinner."

"Excellent plan," Tally called over her shoulder as she headed for her phone.

Chapter 14

Isabelle had given Tally her first wedding planning job in the Caribbean, and then, after the hurricane shut down Vieques Weddings, she'd helped her protégé open her own company on Jekyll Island. She'd moved to an enormous "cabin" on a mountain near Londonderry, Vermont, after Hurricane Maria had rendered her large oceanfront home on Vieques uninhabitable. Between the storm and the looters that rampaged the little island for a year afterward, the only thing left of the multi-million-dollar waterfront villa where she'd held 300-person weddings was the foundation. Even the wiring was gone.

"Hi Isabelle!" Tally answered. "How's Vermont?"

"Vermont is beautiful. I'm just sitting here drinking hot chocolate and watching the snow fall."

"I'm jealous." Tally loved snow, when it was outside and she was inside.

"Well, you won't be jealous for long. I'm calling with good and bad news," Isabelle said. Her tone worried Tally.

"Okay, good news first," Tally told her.

"I sold the Vieques property," Isabelle announced and sighed with relief. Tally let out a whoop of joy.

"Yay! That's fantastic. I'm so happy for you. What a relief!" Between waiting on insurance and trying to sell, Isabelle had been stuck between a financial rock and a hard place for a long time.

"You're telling me. Between battling the insurance company and constantly trying to coordinate with the police there to get paperwork to prove my claims... I'm ready to say goodbye to Vieques and be done with that part of my life."

"I bet you are. So that's not good news, that's amazing news! What was the bad news?"

"I sort of broke my hip," Isabelle told her in a nonchalant tone.

"Oh no." Way to bury the lead, Tally thought. "Are you okay?"

"Oh yes. I'm calling from my hospital room. I slipped on my own front steps and busted my butt. Almost froze to death waiting for the ambulance to get there. Thank God, I had my phone in my coat pocket when I went down."

"That's why I hate you living alone someplace so remote," Tally said, mentally flipping through her calendar to see if she could fly north and help out her friend.

"Well, I broke my right hip and my right ankle," the older woman continued. "They did surgery on both of them at the same time and put me back together with pins and duct tape a couple of days ago. I'm actually feeling much, much better today so I'm hopeful I'll bounce back, but the buyer of my villa made a cash offer and wants to close on the property as soon as the title search clears. And I need your help."

"Sure, anything," Tally was imagining her friend on her butt in the snow, hoping that help would come, and she felt a little sick. "What can I do?"

"Could you go to Vieques as my power of attorney and handle the closing in a couple of weeks?"

"Oh wow. Okay, sure. I can do that for you," Tally promised.

"Check your wedding schedule," she gave Tally the date and the location information. She'd have to be present for a final walk through on Vieques and go to the bank in San Juan to sign the closing documents. "You know how it goes there. It might not happen that day. It could be postponed a few times."

"I'll figure it out. Yaya and Kayla can hold down the fort here for most anything," she assured Isabelle. Her old friend had bailed her out multiple times when she was launching Jekyll Weddings, and she'd move heaven and earth to return the favor.

"I'll pay for your flights, of course," Isabelle said. "And I was planning to make a reservation for you at Hacienda Tamarindo, unless you'd rather stay someplace else. It's under new ownership now so I have no idea what it's like. But the online pics look mostly the same."

"That's fine, I love Hacienda Tamarindo," Tally said. "I'm going to see if Mitch can take off a few days and go with me. He's heard so much about Vieques that I think he'd enjoy seeing it."

"That's a great idea," Isabelle said enthusiastically. "I wasn't loving you going by yourself. I had planned to ask you to go with me when I went because I was feeling a little bit uneasy. I'll buy Mitch's ticket too if you send me the pertinent info. It'll be an engagement gift."

"You already got us a beautiful engagement gift," Tally protested.

"Who said you only get one?"

Chapter 15

Mitch drove Tally over the causeway and the Sidney Lanier bridge, heading into an amazing sunset. The miles of marsh grasses that lined the waterways glittered gold and shape-shifted in the breeze. It went from orange to pink as they made their way to the parking lot of a waterfront restaurant called Marshside Grille. The faded sign on a pole out front made the place look a bit like a dive bar but the inside had withstood the test of time. Tally had a thing for their shrimp quesadillas.

"Okay, before the food comes, tell me why your laundry had a biohazard warning," Tally joked.

"Oh jeez, I just spent the week lying in mud on the Georgia/Florida line."

"Well, that sounds fun. Not."

He explained that the task force had gotten information about a massive drug shipment that was supposed to arrive and where it was crossing into Georgia.

"A swamp?"

"You know how we joke about the difference between the smell of a marsh and a swamp? That's not a joke. Very different experience when you're lying in for hours on end. And there were a lot of snakes and alligators, too."

Tally cringed. "What did you do when you saw an alligator?"

"Nothing. They just walked by us. Some of them looked at us, but none of them even showed the slightest interest when we didn't move," he recalled.

"I don't think I could stay still."

"You would if your life depended on it," Mitch countered.

"I hated you being gone," she told him suddenly, changing the sub-ject. "I missed you."

"I missed you, too. I had zilch signal in the swamp or I would have been bugging the hell out of you the whole time."

"Did you catch the drug runners?"

"Nope. We caught a bunch of illegal immigrants accidentally in-stead, and we think the bruhaha probably scared away the drug guys." He sounded super annoyed.

"That's crazy."

"Yeah well, nobody had been through that area in three days – not one single human, at least – and so when this group of like five Hispan-ic guys comes stomping straight into us, we jumped up and grabbed them. Never occurred to anybody that this was a route for more than just this drug deal," he chuckled. "But everybody had flashlights on and cops were literally coming out of the bushes for five minutes after we stopped them, and we think it's entirely possible that our targets were right behind him. Whether it was a coincidence or they were using them for exactly this purpose, we don't know. But we found evidence of where they'd been hiding on the other side after it all blew up."

When their second round of drinks was delivered to the table – whiskey sour for him and a Captain and Coke for her – Tally told Mitch about Isabelle's call.

"Ankle and hip? Ouch."

"Yeah, big ouch. But that's literally not her biggest worry right now. She's going to be in the hospital another few days and then they're transferring her to a really nice rehab facility near her house. She can't go straight home since she lives alone," she explained.

"Do you want to go up there and help her?" he knew how much Isabelle meant to Tally.

"I'd love to, but she needs something else from me." She told Mitch about the pending villa sale and how she needed to go to Vieques and San Juan to act as Isabelle's power of attorney for the closing.

Tally explained how Isabelle wanted to send them both on a mini vacation combined with doing her this favor, and she pulled up the calendar on her phone at the table so they could start talking dates. The entire process baffled Mitch, who'd never bought a home, much less dealt with Puerto Rican land bureaucracy.

"How can the dates change? If the closing is scheduled for that Monday, why wouldn't it happen if everything else lines up?" He was genuinely curious.

"Well, maybe the woman at the bank who is supposed to print out the final closing documents is out sick," Tally said.

"So why wouldn't somebody else print them?"

"That's not how they do it in Puerto Rico. People are not cross-trained to back each other up. I think it's for job security, honestly. It took me six months to get a driver's license on Vieques because there was only one lady who could administer the written test. She only did it at 11 a.m. on Tuesdays and Thursdays. And for more than a month, her baby was sick on those days, so she didn't come in. Nobody could get a driver's license in Vieques until her little boy got better."

"Seriously?" Mitch's face said he didn't believe her.

"I'm totally not kidding about this. There's one lady on the island who can issue marriage licenses. If she's out sick or on vacation, you can't get paperwork on Vieques. Isabelle had a good relationship with the Demographic Office so she knew the lady's vacation schedule, but when she was sick and we didn't have advance warning, it was a hot mess. A few times, I had to fly to Ceiba with clients and take them to the office in Fajardo to get the paperwork done a day before their weddings."

"That would get annoying really fast. And expensive," he agreed. "I don't think I would like living there."

"It's an amazing place to vacation, and you will love it if you can come. But I don't want to live there again, or any place like Vieques. It was too hard," Tally admitted. "Isabelle said the first few years were an adventure – and I can see that. I was in charge of the cargo ferry shopping trips my first year and I thought it was exciting to take the car ferry and shop on the big island, racing against the clock the whole time. But then it got old. And exhausting."

"I bet."

"Isabelle and I had talked about me taking over more of her business before the storm, but now I'm glad that didn't happen. For a lot of reasons, not the least of which is that I wouldn't be with you right now," she reached over and squeezed his hand.

"I'll talk to my bosses on the task force tomorrow and see if the dates work for them. If I were on patrol, I probably couldn't do a trip on this short notice," he explained in a manner that made it clear he was educating her for life planning purposes. "But while I'm on the task force, things are a lot more flexible. I don't know what they'll say because I don't know what's in the pipeline for that week, but I'll ask. I don't love the idea of you going by yourself if I can't go. Maybe Yaya could go with you if I can't."

"Yaya has to stay here and keep my business running if I go. But don't worry like that. I lived there for years and I'm staying in one of the nicest hotels on the island while I'm there. I won't have any problems. I'm looking forward to visiting a few of my old friends, like Elsie the cake lady. I miss her."

"Hopefully, I can go with you."

After dinner, they went home and pulled out their calendars. Tally had her paper calendar and her laptop open with Outlook up on the screen. Mitch had his small paper calendar that he carried and his phone opened to his calendar. She'd received an email from Isabelle with all the details she needed and they plotted out their trip on the assumption that he'd be able to go with her.

"We'll fly from Jacksonville to San Juan at the crack of dawn on Thursday morning and take a puddle jumper over to Vieques. We'll pick up our rental car and I'll take you on a tour of the island. Friday is villa paperwork first thing in the morning and then we'll have the whole weekend to play. The closing is supposed to happen on Monday afternoon in San Juan. If it's postponed, I have to stay a couple more days, but you could go straight back if you have to work."

The look on his face said that wasn't going to happen and Tally didn't argue because she wasn't thrilled about going to Puerto Rico alone. She hadn't been back since the storm and she thought she might have some PTSD kicking in as she thought about her return. She wondered if she'd run into Eduardo while they were there and decided she'd like to avoid having to introduce him to Mitch, if she could help it. She wanted to take Mitch out to see the biobay, but she wouldn't be booking it with the company Eduardo still worked for. There were plenty of companies that offered kayak tours of the sparkling bioluminescent water.

"Hey Tally, while we have our calendars out, how about we set a wedding date?" Mitch suggested gently. Her head snapped up when she heard him.

"Right now?"

"Why not? I need to run that date by my bosses, too. Why not kill two birds with one stone?"

Tally knew he was right. They had a fairly-solid guest list worked out – thanks to his mother and grandmother - and they chatted about the events they wanted to host for their guests. They wanted to offer some additional things for the people coming from out of town and had talked about renting a trolley for a tour of the historic district. But they hadn't been able to lock down a date.

"I'd like it to be sooner, than later," Mitch said, looking Tally in the eye.

"Me too," she agreed, wondering if she was crazy when she thought about her schedule. Then Isabelle's advice about relationships being "glass balls" helped her make a decision.

"Okay let's do it. I think it needs to be in a time window when I don't have any big weddings booked for two weeks solid. At least 10 days." He watched her clicking away at her computer and didn't interrupt. It was the closest they gotten to picking a date and he wasn't going to risk distracting her.

"Okay so we have a few options," she began. "But ugh, it's like we can do it right away or next year."

"You're a victim of your own success. Can I look at it with you?" he asked.

"Sure," Tally turned the laptop so Mitch could see the full image of the 12-month calendar with weeks blocked out where she already had event deposits.

"Holy shit, you weren't kidding! I'm marrying a rockstar," he declared. "May I?" he asked before pulling the laptop closer and comparing it with his own calendar.

"So we could do February? Nah, too soon," Mitch answered himself. "What's with the four-week block at the end of May, beginning of June?"

"Oh, Abby and I had talked about them taking a trip with us for our birthdays this year, instead of her coming here. But we hadn't nailed anything down, so I was keeping the calendar blocked for now. I can add a bunch of elopements to the calendar and other little stuff once I know which week we'd be gone," she explained.

"So why don't we get married then?"

"On my birthday?" she asked, a horrified look on her face.

"Not on your birthday," he replied quickly. "But somewhere in that time block. Because otherwise, it looks like we're screwed until the Christmas holidays."

Tally knew he wasn't wrong and she chided herself for worrying if it was enough time. She could plan and execute her own wedding in a week, if the guests would actually come that fast. Six months was enough lead time for a destination wedding, even though she advised clients to send their save-the-dates out as far ahead as a year. Most of their guests were local anyway. And she had a feeling that a Durham wedding on Jekyll Island would be the event of the season.

Chapter 16

The weather on Saturday was perfect for Alita and Juan's wedding day. Kayla had been by the wedding venue to drop off bouquets and check in with the bride in person. She'd reported to Tally that the DJ and the caterer providing the bar had set everything up according to the timeline, and there was nothing to worry about on their end.

Tally would have let Kayla run the wedding on her own if not for the Christian/Persian double wedding ceremony element. It was better to have both sets of their hands on deck with so many details to coordinate. There wasn't a big service staff to ask for help like at most weddings.

"I will say a prayer and then instruct them each to taste the honey, the nuts, etc." Alita's father gave Tally and Kayla a rundown on the ceremony he would perform. "The doves will be in their cage on the small table you will set up."

"I've got that table and tablecloth ready so we'll get it moved over here when you guys are all down on the beach for that ceremony," Kayla assured him. "After the ceremony on the beach is finished, Alita and Juan will walk back up the aisle, toward the stairway back to the villa, and you will all follow the bride and groom. I suggest you get to the front of the group so you have a minute to make sure you like the table setup before everyone is assembled."

"Please make sure it's exactly like I want it," he said.

"He set it up on the kitchen table inside the villa exactly as we're supposed to put it on the table out here," Kayla told Tally. "I took a picture. But we'll just move that stuff from that table to this table exactly as he had it."

"Sounds well thought out," Tally smiled. "Now the father of the bride needs to go get himself dressed because it's almost time for him to walk Alita down the aisle," she teased, gesturing for the bride's father to get moving.

Just then, a harried bridesmaid came running out of the villa in search of Kayla. Alita was having a problem with her wedding gown.

"Want me to handle it?" Tally offered.

"Would you mind? I see guests arriving, and without staff, I need to point them toward the beach. Unless you'd rather do that."

"You know what is supposed to be happening out here, so I'm going to go fix the bride," Tally and Kayla both laughed. "That sounded bad. I'm going to go assist the bride-to-be into her dress. Text if you need me."

"Divide and conquer," Kayla joked as her boss walked away toward the villa.

Alita was in her dress, but it wasn't even beginning to close in the back. She was wedged in so tightly that it didn't make any sense. She was tiny. Tally almost laughed but the bride was near tears so she thought better of it.

"Oh, I see the problem," Tally lied in a happy voice. "This is easy." She hoped she was right. But Isabelle had taught her that when a dress doesn't seem to fit, they probably put it on wrong.

She approached Alita carefully. "Let me help you take this off and we'll start over. But give me a second to make sure everything is unhooked so we don't rip something."

"I already heard something rip," the bride said sadly.

"Well, then let's hope it was nothing anybody can see. My Lord, Alita, this gown has a million layers of skirt."

Tally got the bride giggling as she examined the problem and carefully pulled the dress over her head, after first tying a scarf over Alita's hair to protect the updo. Somehow Alita had gotten into her dress between the lining and the skirt, rather than inside the actual lining. As soon as she was out of it, Tally orchestrated the bride carefully stepping back into it – between the correct layers – and viola! It zipped up without a problem.

She left the girls celebrating with the bride and joined Kayla at the top of the steps to the beach where she was watching guests navigate the steep, narrow staircase to the sand.

"Crisis averted?" Kayla asked.

"She was in between layers of tulle instead of inside the lining."

"Well that explains it," she chuckled. "Easy fix at least."

"I think they came and got us just in time because the lining was starting to tear where it was being pulled away from the skirt," Tally said. "But it's fine and you can't see any problems on the dress with her wearing it so it's a win in my book. She looks gorgeous, by the way."

"Her skin tone is amazing with that blush pink gown," Kayla agreed.

"I love really pale pink gowns," Tally agreed.

"You thinking of wearing pink?" her friend asked.

"I hadn't been, honestly."

"Maybe you should," Kayla suggested, as the father-of-the-bride reappeared beside them wearing a summer suit and looking far better than he had before.

The Christian part of the wedding ceremony flowed easily. The trickiest part was watching Alita descend that staircase after they convinced her to ditch the heels – she wouldn't be wearing them on the beach anyway – at the top.

"I wanted the shoes to show in my entrance pictures," she'd whined. Her photographer had quickly jumped in to volunteer to shoot pictures of the bride on the staircase in her heels and gown after the ceremony, when it could be safely staged.

Disaster averted, Kayla sent the bride down the aisle. Alita made a beautiful entrance and took her father's arm at the bottom of the staircase. It wasn't wide enough for two people at the same time. The wedding planners watched until Alita had taken Juan's hand in front of the minister they'd hired to perform the ceremony. Reverend Ray was an old hat at this and they didn't need to worry once he was in control.

Tally and Kayla carried the tables they'd stashed in the bushes and set them up. They draped the tablecloths Kayla had brought and then carefully carried all the small bowls holding the elements of the Persian wedding ceremony outside to recreate the setup.

"You get the doves," Tally told Kayla.

"Hell no, I don't do birds. You do it. It's your company." Tally laughed because Kayla rarely pushed back. "I'm not kidding, Tally."

"I believe you." Tally walked over to the bird cage to survey the situation.

The deck was a gross mess from whatever they'd been feeding the birds. She wasn't going to clean it up because she'd specifically line-itemed the handling of live animals in her contract, and she was crossing that line by just moving the damned birds for the ceremony. But she did it because it needed to be done.

By the time they were finished on the beach, the Persian ceremony was set up and waiting. Alita's aunts had skipped the first ceremony while they set the long table on the porch for the wedding party, complete with a Barbie doll that looked just like Alita, sitting next to the bride's pink plastic dinner plate. But everybody from the house was out in the yard when the bride's father began the ceremony in his native language.

It was really pretty, and Tally took pictures. The doves were the grand finale of the Persian ceremony, so to speak, and when it was time to release them, the father of the bride moved their cage from the smaller table on the side and put it on the big table. That was when Kayla started filming on her phone. He said some more prayers and then opened the cage, handing one bird to his daughter and the other to her new groom. Then he said another prayer and gestured for them to release the birds. The guests stood silent around them, watching in anticipation.

And that was when things went sideways.

When the groom threw his dove up in the air, he used more force than was necessary and disoriented the bird. It went flipping up into the air and then dropped like a rock, only regaining its equilibrium in time to avoid smashing into the ground. Then it landed on the grass and sat there looking at the groom accusingly while the wedding planners tried not to laugh.

Alita's bird had flown up in the air in the way Tally had imagined it was supposed to happen, but then it didn't fly away. First, it landed in a nearby tree and stared at them. Then it flew back over to the porch where it had lived for the past couple of days and sat down on the bride's plate next to the Barbie doll. Its butt-hurt mate spotted it and joined it on the dinner table, pooping on the groom as he flew over the wedding party.

An old woman, one of Alita's aunts who'd been in the kitchen all day, stood next to Tally and Kayla as the chaos unfolded. She muttered in her own language.

"Hmmm?" Tally asked, not looking away from her clients.

"I told them not to feed those fucking birds," the old woman replied in perfect, unaccented English. "If you feed them, they won't fly away because why would they want to leave. I warned my brother not to let the children feed them once they arrived, but nobody listened to me..." she resumed muttering in another tongue.

"Oh wow," Kayla said and looked at Tally. They both cracked up. "Now what?" she asked as the second bird strutted down the middle of the dinner table.

"It's not often I can say 'this isn't our problem' during an event, but seriously, this is not our disaster to fix. Let's go over and check on the music. He can probably turn that up a bit so it can be heard over here for dinner," Tally said. And then she led Kayla away from the table. The aunts had surrounded it and were trying to chase the doves away. The birds were winning that war.

Chapter 17

Tally laughed til she had tears rolling down her cheeks as she described the disastrous ending to Alita and Juan's ceremony to Mitch later than night.

"We hid for the rest of the night, someplace we could keep an eye on things but where they couldn't easily find us. The guests didn't understand why we weren't dealing with the birds even though the bride's family knew it was their problem. Since the meal wasn't catered, we had no reason to be anywhere near the porch during dinner. Kayla and I hid on the pool deck."

"And where are the birds now?" Mitch asked, afraid of the answer.

"We put them back in their cage," she laughed. "The DJ took them home with him. He has a cousin that's into birds or something."

Technically, his fiancée shouldn't be letting her clients release birds in a state park. It was very illegal, even if she didn't get caught, and he'd planned to talk to her about it. He wasn't sure he needed to now. He had a feeling she wouldn't ever allow another bird at a wedding again.

"I need to go by their villa when they check out and take a hose to the deck if they didn't clean up better where that birdcage was."

"I thought they paid a deposit," Mitch countered.

"They did. But that doesn't matter. If they left a big-ass mess, that house will not love having our weddings in the future. And some bride with a two-pound dog won't be allowed to have her precious puppy stay for her wedding a year from now because of birdshit. Unintended consequences of one couple's wedding can impact all future events. So, I'm going to go clean it up so it's not an issue. Even if it makes me gag."

"Is that your way of saying you need my help?" he laughed, reading between the lines.

"I'd love your help!" she answered the question she wished had been asked with a big grin he couldn't turn down. "Bright and early Monday morning. I'll buy you breakfast afterwards if we're not too grossed out to eat."

"The things I do for you," he shook his head but he was chuckling. "Speaking of which, I got the days off to go to Vieques with you. I booked two extra just in case we need them, but my commander was pretty cool about it. Everybody's nice to the guy who was wounded."

Tally rolled her eyes but didn't think he was funny. Mitch had been wounded in the line of duty a year earlier. It had been one of the scariest experiences of her life. He'd had his pick of jobs when he was cleared to go back to work as a trooper and he'd chosen to return to the drug interdiction task force that he was working on when he was shot. Tally had not been thrilled but she'd kept it to herself. He loved his job. He loved her. She wasn't going to make him choose which he loved more.

"Great. I'll let Isabelle know so we can buy the plane tickets," Tally popped off a text knowing that if her friend was asleep, her phone would be off.

Isabelle replied a few minutes later, sending Tally a picture of the front and back of her credit cards and instructions to book their trip. To Tally, that meant Isabelle felt too crappy to book it herself and that made her worry. But when she said as much to Mitch, he told her she was reading too much into it.

"Maybe that's true, or maybe Isabelle is on pain meds and it's almost midnight and she trusts you enough to give you her card to just take care of it," he suggested. "Don't borrow things to worry about when they haven't actually happened yet. You have enough real things racing around in your head."

"True dat," she agreed, trying to get into a lighter mood.

When they climbed into bed a little while later, Tally brought her laptop and worked on planning their trip while Mitch watched "Live PD." It cracked her up that he worked in law enforcement and preferred to watch shows that portrayed his job. There was always something like that on TV.

"Hey Tally, I got some other good news today, too," Mitch announced after muting the TV for a commercial. "I can have the last week of May and the first week of June off. So we can get married on May 30th."

"Oh wow, that makes it super real, doesn't it?"

"That okay with you?" Mitch asked, pulling her close to him.

Tally leaned back over to shut the laptop and then turned to her fiancé.

"It's more than just 'okay,' it's perfect," she said. "It's also overwhelming and I'm feeling a lot. Not bad things just a lot of things." She turned to try to hide the tears welling up in her eyes. They were happy tears but she still felt stupid.

He nodded like he understood exactly what she was thinking, even though Tally knew he hadn't the faintest clue. He pulled her close and kissed her, and the kiss led to other things, and wedding planning was forgotten until morning.

Chapter 18

Mitch marveled as Tally slept in her center airplane seat for the entire flight to Puerto Rico. She'd told him that flying knocked her out – ever since she was a baby in her car seat in the back of her father's twin Comanche airplane – but he hadn't expected her to fall asleep on takeoff.

In fairness, he was pretty sure she hadn't slept more than a few hours in the nights leading up to their trip. He'd had some more overnight undercover work in the meantime so he wasn't home to give her a hard time about working too much. But still, when she reclined her seat back the minute the big jet lifted off the ground (against the rules, the state trooper in him noted wryly), she conked out right away and hadn't moved much since, except to steal more of the arm rest.

He gently woke her up when the lady in the window seat opened the shade as they approached San Juan. It was bright and sunny out and Mitch got more excited for the adventure than he had been during the planning. They'd gotten it all done and were on their way and it was time for him to relax and take his brain out of cop mode for a few days. Tally had promised to be a bride instead of a wedding planner, whatever that meant.

The air conditioning was out in the terminal where they had to wait for the Cape Air flight over to Vieques. Tally assured him that the trek through the stuffy terminal and long, hot wait for their flight at the janky gate would be worth it when he saw Vieques.

"This is always the worst part of the trip," she said. "And it's even worse if you're taking the ferry from Fajardo to Vieques. That trip takes all day."

"Why would people opt for the ferry then?" he asked.

"The ferry costs them a few bucks and the flights are at least $200 roundtrip now out of San Juan airport, sometimes twice that. Used to be you could fly into the little airports cheaper, but Vieques Airlink isn't running as many flights since Hurricane Maria."

"I didn't realize this part of the trip was so expensive," Mitch said. "Isn't it a short flight?" He was starting to wish he'd paid more attention to the details when she'd talked about the struggles of getting to and from Vieques.

"About 20 minutes. But like I said, if you don't do it this way, it takes all day. By taking a puddle jumper, we'll be on a beach this afternoon."

"If you say so."

"I do," Tally assured him. Then she pulled out some maps and materials from her backpack that he remembered seeing on their counter, and they spent the rest of their wait reviewing what was where and how they'd be spending their down time. This time, Mitch paid attention.

The flight departed late, and if a passenger wasn't paying attention, he'd likely be left behind, Mitch thought to himself as he followed Tally down a gangway that led to a staircase to the ground. The passengers hoofed it across the tarmac to a small airplane with Cape Air painted on its fuselage, and then the gate agent who had led them out there took their purses and carry-ons away from them. Tally had warned him about that and it had played into his decision not to bring a gun along on the trip. He was unlikely to run into anybody he'd arrested in Puerto Rico, so he shouldn't have any problems.

He didn't like it one bit when the pilot told Tally to sit in the co-pilot's seat as they were boarding. She'd warned him about that, too. The pilot always put the smallest woman, or the prettiest girl, in the co-pilot's seat. Allegedly, it had to do with balancing the plane but Mitch knew better.

He was seated behind the pilot and had a spectacular view. Tally did a lot of leaning back and screaming to him over the sound of the propellers to identify famous spots as they flew over them. She'd pointed out the beach and kioskos at Luquillo, the El Conquistador resort on a cliff, and the former Roosevelt Roads Navy base in Ceiba that had been shut down after the government of Puerto Rico kicked the U.S. military off Vieques Island.

The Navy used the eastern end of the little island as a bombing range for 50 years and Tally said they'd probably never be able to safely use the beach on that end of Vieques in their lifetimes. It was a Superfund EPA cleanup site that provided a lot of jobs now.

They landed at an airport that was only a little bigger than the one on Jekyll Island, and then collected their bags from the world's tiniest baggage carousel. Mitch couldn't stop laughing.

"What's the point of that?" he asked Tally.

"I agree it's funny but careful with the laughing and pointing because Viequenses think their island is pretty perfect and they get offended easily," she warned.

"Really?"

"Really. There are a few Facebook groups for residents, since there's no local newspaper or radio station, and it gets ugly sometimes. At least once a week, somebody tells a gringo to 'go home' after they complain about something totally understandable like their trash not getting picked up for the third week in a row, or the fact that there is no Dr. Pepper to be found on the entire island."

"Ah, First World problems," Mitch could understand why it bothered the locals to be compared. "I'll be careful and more thoughtful," he promised.

"I don't know how many people we'll see that I know, or rather, that are happy to see me," she warned him, not for the first time.

"Tally, relax. I'm not judging you based on how this trip goes. I'm just excited to be here seeing the famous Vieques in person with you. Do you realize this is our first big trip together?" he asked.

She paused and laughed. "You're right. I hadn't thought about it that way."

"We hardly have to do anything for Isabelle while we're here so let's just have a really great time. Don't think about the negative stuff unless we encounter it, and then we'll deal with it then," he said as their suitcases finally appeared on the little ramp.

When they got outside, Mitch watched as Tally negotiated a ride in a taxi van she called a "publico" to get them to the rental car agency. She used Spanish and seemed comfortable in the language, which intrigued him because she rarely spoke it with Yaya. When he mentioned it to her, she said she felt out of practice.

"Yaya's English is 100 times better than my Spanish so we never use it. Bad habit. I should ask her to practice with me. I'll probably have to pay her more though," she joked.

There were horses grazing on the grass around the airport driveway and Mitch pointed them out to Tally with a confused look.

"I told you there are wild horses all over the island. You'll see." And he did.

The publico passed a lot of storm destruction on the way to the rental car place, but nothing worse than the remains of the wall around the W Hotel. It looked like a kid had kicked down blocks.

"Isabelle's house was inside that compound," Tally pointed as they drove by. "You'll see what's left of it tomorrow." He noticed his fiancée was not smiling as they drove across her old stomping grounds. There were random horses on both sides of the road munching grass. Many of them looked too thin to be healthy but Mitch withheld commenting on it in front of the taxi driver.

The rental car place cracked Mitch up. It was called JoJo's and it was located on a residential street. JoJo ran the business out of his mom's garage. There was an Avis and a few other places on Vieques they could have used, but Jeep rentals from them ran $90 day. JoJo's was $35 a day in cash. The tires were sketchy but he'd switch out the vehicle if you had problems, according to Tally.

He was amused to find that the rental car place doubled as a movie rental store. Apparently, people in Puerto Rico still watched DVDs, which made sense when he thought about the Internet streaming problems Tally had complained about. Mitch stood out front with their luggage while Tally walked into the store, waving hello but not stopping to chat with several people drinking beers and eating candy bars at a concrete picnic table in front of the house.

She was back with the keys less than three minutes later.

"What about paperwork?" he asked.

"There's no paperwork. We call JoJo if we have a problem. His number is in my phone," she replied like taking a rental car without doing a bunch of paperwork and an inspection was perfectly normal.

He loaded their luggage into the back of a less-than-totally-clean black Jeep Wrangler that had a soft top but no window coverings.

"Hope it doesn't rain," Mitch remarked.

"It will," Tally said. "But it dries fast. Want me to drive so you can look around?"

"Sure, give me the tour," he said and climbed into the passenger seat. He noticed horses grazing in a few front yards around JoJo's but none of them appeared to be fenced in. There was a lot of poop in the road too, and he mentioned it to Tally.

"We're not in Jekyll anymore, Toto," she told him, laughing.

Tally made sure they had plenty of gas in the Jeep, something that was never certain with a Caribbean rental car, and then she drove to the far west end of Vieques, the area that had been the base of Camp Garcia.

She took Mitch down windy roads with overgrown vegetation and showed him bunkers the Navy had used to store all the munitions for the North Atlantic fleet. The municipality used them for storage now, and a number of people had taken shelter inside them during the bigger storms over the years if their houses weren't concrete. It wasn't pleasant but it was safe. And there were horses everywhere.

She showed Mitch her favorite spot at Green Beach – also known as Punta Arenas before the military took over and renamed everything – on the western tip of the island. She was sad to see the erosion at what used to be a favorite snorkeling and diving spot. Some of the picnic cabanas the Navy had built along the cove were actually under water now, and she pointed them out to him beneath the surface.

Tally drove back to the middle of the island and took Mitch on a quick tour through the capital, Isabel Segunda. She pointed out the grocery stores – both owned by the same family – and several bars and restaurants where they'd held events for clients. She also showed him the cat corner where the old lady fed so many feral cats that there were hundreds of them waiting outside her house at all times. Totally freaky, he'd agreed. He'd made her stop the Jeep to let him take a picture of a horse standing in line in front of the only bank's ATM like he was waiting to use it.

She showed Mitch the lighthouse and the fort. where she'd had to go to get a phone signal after the storm. Then they'd taken the road out of town, past the hospital that had been condemned since Hurricane Maria. They were supposed to be building a new one, but it was in the hands of the government of Puerto Rico which Tally said meant it could take forever.

Mitch gasped when they drove over a hill in Destino and he got his first view of the eastern end of the island, the former Camp Garcia bombing range. Miles of white sand beach along a shoreline that seemed to go on forever.

As they drove, Tally explained that the eastern end of the island had been the Atlantic Fleet Weapons Training Area for many years. Back then, the locals had been able to enjoy the beaches where there were no bombing exercises going on. Then an Italian pilot on his virgin bombing run killed a civilian security guard who wasn't where he was supposed to be at the Observation Post and anti-military protesters went nuts. The protesters won and the Navy pulled out of Vieques. But the Navy claimed that without Vieques and its bombing range, there was no point in the United States maintaining the giant Roosevelt Roads Navy base in Ceiba. So, they closed that down too, and returned the land to the government of Puerto Rico. Lots of jobs were lost.

Camp Garcia had been officially renamed the Vieques Federal Wildlife Refuge and the beaches returned to the names they'd had before the military labeled them by color. Tally said they'd always be Red Beach, Blue Beach, etcetera to her, but she respected Viequenses heritage and called them by their correct names in front of locals. Red Beach was "Caracas" and Blue Beach was "Bahia de la Chiva." She told Mitch they'd go there another day as she passed the gate and headed toward the south side of the island.

There was nobody at the guard booth at the entrance to Sun Bay, the municipal beach that Tally told Mitch was her favorite. They drove in through an open gate – Tally said one side was always left open – and took the sandy road along the beach. He loved the many shades of blue in the crystal-clear waters.

"This isn't what it used to look like," she explained sadly, as if the scene weren't something out of a movie. "It's missing about 500 palm trees. You can see they're trying to grow more, but it will never be the same." She pointed to what Mitch had thought were bushes on the beach and he saw they were actually baby palm trees. He was more fascinated by the naked dead palm trees that stuck out of the ground at random places along their route. The Jekyll Island Authority arborist would have a fit if he saw them.

Tally drove them through Esperanza, the tourist town on the southern side of the island. She pointed out the Malecon – a concrete boardwalk that had taken a beating and was still being repaired. She pointed to a few bars where she'd done events and an empty lot that used to hold a breakfast place. She waved to the owners of Lazy Jack's as they passed by.

The road exited the little beach town and wound along the coast. Mitch had to hold on as Tally whipped a quick left turn into a sand and gravel driveway. The rutted road led up to the parking lot of Hacienda Tamarindo, the bed and breakfast where they'd be staying. From the top of the hill, there was a beautiful view all the way to the Caribbean Sea.

"I used to want to get married at this hotel," she told Mitch.

He bent over and planted a kiss on her lips. "I think it's time to make some new memories here."

Chapter 19

By the time Tally and Mitch were checked into Room 5 at the beautiful bed and breakfast, the sky was turning dark.

"What happened?" Mitch asked when he opened the French doors onto their patio and saw the sky.

"It's like Jekyll," Tally explained. "Except it usually moves a lot faster here. Which is weird because Vieques is a lot bigger. But anyway, you can't write off the day for this – it could still be sunny on the other side of the island. Let's get unpacked and go get lunch before we go to the beach," she suggested.

Tally drove them back into Esperanza.

"I'd take you to Bellybuttons," she said on the way while she pointed to her former favorite lunch spot. "But it's gone."

She pulled the Jeep into a driveway beside Duffy's that he hadn't even noticed and found a parking spot behind the building. She said she didn't recognize anyone working behind the big bar in the middle of the place, but also explained that it had been sold to a new owner just a few days before the storm.

"The guy who owned it was a legacy on Vieques – his dad was THE Duffy. Mikey Duffy still has another restaurant open here called Tin Box – we'll go there this weekend. His food is spectacular. He used to cater for Isabelle all the time," Tally told Mitch as they split a plate of jerk chicken wings.

"The wings are good. I'm looking forward to the mahi sandwich. I can't believe you wanted to split one. I'm eating my whole sandwich," she knew Mitch was trying to lighten the mood but she couldn't help feeling a little bit weird about being back on Vieques. She kept looking around expecting to see people she knew. There were some familiar faces but not many.

When the waiter returned to their table, Tally ordered a pina colada in hopes that it would help her loosen up.

The rain stopped after lunch so they strolled along what was left of the Malecon. She taught him about the history of the island as they walked – pointing out the old sugar cane pier - and several spots where funny things had happened. Trying to explain the crazy guy who lived in a shack by the auto parts store and rode a bicycle all over the island with puppies and piglets in a trailer behind him was difficult so Tally gave up.

"I'll have to show you his place when we're on the other side of the island," she said, giggling. "That's the best way I can explain Ramache."

Tally said hello to everybody who recognized her but only stopped to have conversations with a few people. She felt like she was holding her breath the entire time, waiting to run into Eduardo or his mean little sister, Anna Maria.

There was a crack of thunder and the heavens opened on them just as they got to the far end of the Malecon. "Oh shit. Run," Tally yelled before taking off back the way they come, splashing as she went. They were both soaked through by the time they got to the Jeep, which didn't have windows to protect them anyway. And the wind was starting to whip up.

"Want to go back to the hotel and get dry?" Tally asked.

"I have several ideas of things we can do at the hotel to keep us out of the rain," he teased.

When they got back to Hacienda Tamarindo, they left a wet trail through the lobby to their room. The hotel was largely open to the elements on all sides, except where there were rooms, so it was wet before Tally and Mitch got there, and there was a housekeeper pushing a mop around to get the worst puddles. Tally waved and smiled at her and the maid smiled and winked.

Once in their room, Tally and Mitch helped each other strip off their soaking clothes. They jumped into the shower together shivering. They'd accidentally left the air conditioning on in their room while they were gone and it was brutally cold on their wet skin. However, the beautifully-tiled shower had not been designed for two people to comfortably use. Once they were warm, Mitch did the honorable thing and stepped out so that Tally could wash her hair without elbowing him in the stomach. He stayed in the steamy bathroom, wrapped in a towel, chatting with her while she showered because he didn't want to re-enter the frozen tundra of the bedroom to adjust the temperature.

Tally had made dinner reservations for them next door at the Inn on the Blue Horizon. She planned dozens of weddings for Isabelle there on the lawn and she wanted to show it to Mitch so he could put some of her more ridiculous stories into context.

"See the little cottage over there," Tally pointed across the lawn. They were sitting at a table on the porch with a view of the Caribbean. There were only a few hotel rooms in the inn's main building. The rest of the rooms were in casitas sprinkled across the property, facing the water, in a U-shape.

"That's where that couple got into a fight," she knew she'd told him the story before but Mitch looked at her blankly. "The bride and groom got into a physical altercation over there the night before the wedding and the manager called Isabelle and said get over here and separate them or I have to call the police," she reminded him.

"Oh right," he chuckled.

"So she called me and the interns and we all jumped into our cars and came over here to sort the mess out," she continued. "The interns arrived first but they wisely waited for us in the parking lot. Then we all trudged down that path to their room. They were having a slap fight when we arrived."

"Did they still get married?" Mitch asked.

"Yeah, they did. It was nuts. Everybody on our staff was like 'are you freaking kidding me' and Isabelle kept reminding us that we get paid for making beautiful weddings, not deciding if people should get married. She's right about that and I've had to bite my tongue a few times on Jekyll already. It's a good policy."

Chapter 20

Everything except the bars along the Malecon shut down early on Vieques Island, so Tally and Mitch drove down to Sun Bay after dinner and went for a moonlight walk along the water. There was nobody around and the sky was clear.

"I thought we could see a lot of stars in Georgia, but this is wild," he said as he picked out yet another visible constellation.

"There's a lot more light at home than around here. That's the biggest difference. The stars aren't as bright in San Juan as they are on Vieques," Tally explained.

"Makes sense."

"Wait til you see the biobay tomorrow night. It's too bad there's going to be some moon, but it may be cloudy. The darker it is, the more the water sparkles. It's wild." Tally had been gushing about the biobay to Mitch from the moment they started planning. She'd told him about swimming in the biobay with Eduardo and his friends – totally illegal but who was going to stop them – and how a trail of light followed everything that moved in the water.

"There are only seven biobays left in the world and Vieques has the brightest," she bragged.

Tally and Mitch were going to take a legal tour in a two-man clear-bottom kayak the next night, guided by one of the other well-established companies on the island where she still had a friend. Tally had called Mindy a week earlier to figure out when the best time to book would be for the least likely chance of running into her ex. All the companies launched boats from the same beach and the biobay wasn't that big. Mindy told her to take the last tour on Saturday night because the senior guys usually made the younger guys do that tour and all the cleanup afterwards. That meant Eduardo would probably be sitting at one of the local bars drinking when they climbed into their kayak.

Tally's alarm woke them up the next morning in time to get to breakfast. She swore Hacienda Tamarindo had the best breakfasts on the entire island and they were included with the nightly rate. All Mitch and Tally had to do was get presentable and arrive before breakfast ended at 10.

It was a beautiful day and Tally put on her bathing suit with a cover up and flip flops to go to breakfast. Mitch followed her lead and put on a t-shirt and swim trunks. They went upstairs to the pretty patio surrounded by blooming purple bougainvillea and drank coffee as they ate bowls of fruit and waited for the special of the day. After they were seated, the waitress delivered a cooler to their table. It had their room number on it.

"I forgot to tell you that I ordered a picnic lunch for us to take to the beach," Tally explained after she thanked the woman who brought it. "As you saw yesterday, it's almost impossible to grab a quick lunch anywhere or pick up sandwiches in under an hour, so this is the best plan for a long beach day. I got two sandwiches – one is chicken salad and I don't remember what the other one was. You can pick one or we can go halfsies."

She dove into her omelet when it arrived and it was as good as she remembered. She was eating the last bites when she realized that Mitch was staring at her. She put her fork down.

"What? Do I have food on my face?" she asked.

"No," Mitch laughed. "You're fine. I was just thinking about how amazing you are. We only found out about this trip a few weeks ago and you have everything all organized perfectly. Right down to our pre-ordered picnic lunch. You are wonderful and hilarious."

"I can't help it," she laughed with him and blushed. "It's the planner in me. Makes me insane to not know what the plan for the day is. I mean I can enjoy a slow beach day if that's what we planned to do, I just want to know what I'm doing when I get up in the morning. I'm not very good at winging it."

"Well, as the one who benefits from your OCD planning habits, I disagree. I think you're fabulous at it. I just hope you'll relax since there's nothing else to do here. You're not going to work on the beach are you?"

"Oh hell no. I only brought my laptop in case Kayla has an emergency and I have to get into a file for her. I don't plan to unzip the bag if I don't absolutely have to. I have a bunch of books that I want to read on the beach. I've been saving them up," she bragged.

"What does that mean?"

"When I lived here, I discovered that Kindle Unlimited was my best friend. I didn't even have a TV most of the time – we just watched stuff via WiFi on our tablets and used the laptop for a big screen if we wanted to watch together," she said. Mitch laughed but stopped when he realized she wasn't kidding.

"Right," Tally continued. "So anyway, getting books in English on Vieques is expensive – pretty much have to order them shipped in or get lucky at one of the bars that has a shelf available to swap. Kindle Unlimited saved my budget and kept me from going crazy. And paper books were always reserved for reading on the beach since I couldn't see my screen outside in the sun."

"Interesting. I didn't know you were a hoarder," he joked.

"It was a habit I got into and I continued it on Jekyll because paper books are still expensive. I still read on my iPad at home and reserve the books for beach or pool time. I know you think I'm nuts.

"Oh, absolutely." Mitch confirmed. "But not because of your weird book-hoarding habits."

Tally and Mitch left shortly after breakfast. The hotel provided big fluffy beach towels, chairs, umbrellas, and coolers for beverages, in addition to the backpack style cooler that held their lunch. There was a big ice machine near the exit to the parking lot where guests were encouraged to help themselves. Mitch loaded the Jeep, which had, miraculously, dried in the morning sun, while Tally put beer and sodas into the Igloo and covered them with ice.

"Okay, so first stop is Isabelle's villa to meet up with her realtor," Tally said. "Then we'll head out to Red and Blue beaches today. The stuff on the wildlife refuge is always a zoo on weekends because San Juanerros come over with boats and jet skis, so we'll do Sun Bay tomorrow to avoid that."

"Feels a little strange to go to a business meeting in a bathing suit," Mitch said.

"This is Vieques. Anything more than flip flops and a t-shirt is considered overdressed. We're fine."

He knew she hadn't been kidding when they pulled up in what used to be Isabelle's driveway and he saw the realtor was wearing shorts with a jog bra and had brought along her dog. He was amused until he looked over and saw Tally's face.

Her reaction to returning to a place she had loved and spent so much of her time, only to find it truly gone, had knocked the wind out of her. "It didn't look this bad when I left," she said softly.

Isabelle had tried to warn her – she'd said that all that was left in the pictures she'd seen were the concrete pads in the ground. Looters were like vultures. They'd picked the empty property clean until there was nothing left.

Mitch reached over and squeezed her hand as the realtor approached their Jeep. "You okay?"

Tally took a deep breath. "Yeah. It's just hard to see it like this. I was supposed to own it someday." Isabelle had planned to slowly turn the company over to Tally, allowing her to invest part of her earnings to become part owner. After the storm, she'd been smart enough to realize that Vieques wouldn't be ready to host tourists or wedding guests for a long time and she'd shut her wedding planning business down. It had broken Tally's heart, but if it hadn't happened, she wouldn't be standing here holding Mitch's hand.

"God shuts a door but opens a window," she told him, squeezing his hand tighter. "Let's get this over with and go to the beach."

The "walk-through" part of the exchange was easy because there was nothing but ruins to step around. Tally took a video of it for Isabelle to keep, signed a couple of things, and got a page of written instructions from the realtor on where to be and what to bring for the closing on Monday afternoon in San Juan. She and Mitch were catching a Vieques Airlink flight from Vieques to Isla Grande Airport in Old San Juan, next to the port where the big cruise ships docked. It was just a few minutes from her favorite hotel – El Convento – a renovated 400-year-old convent with a roof deck view of the beautiful coastline. They would stay there for two nights and explore Old San Juan.

It would take half a day just to walk around El Morro, the historic fort on a cliff at the entrance to the San Juan port. If the closing got bumped by a few hours or a whole day, they would just work around it and do their touring when they weren't busy. There were beaches on the big island, too, of course. But Tally had been spoiled by Vieques and Jekyll and she avoided the crowds on the beaches in front of the big hotels on the Condado and along Isla Verde. She and Mitch would stick to the shops and museums in the historic part of the city.

Tally took Mitch to Secret Beach – also known as Playa Prieta – for the afternoon.

"It was a 'secret' until they put it on the freakin tourist map," she ranted. "Now it's just a cool place to go but you can't get topless or have sex like the old days."

"Well, that's a bummer," Mitch agreed, imagining the scene in his head.

"It's still fun," she promised. "It's beautiful. It's a super shallow quiet little cove but it's also really cool because, in August when you can't get relief in the water because the ocean feels like a warm bathtub, there's a cold current that runs into Secret Beach. I've spent entire afternoons chasing the cold spots here." She laughed at the memory but it was real. People in Georgia whined about the heat in August and Tally just rolled her eyes at them. Jekyll Island was comfy compared to Vieques.

Mitch played tourist as Tally told him more about the island.

"There were protesters camped out here for a couple of years," she explained as they rolled through the gates into the former Navy bombing range. "But that was all over with before I ever got here. That leads to the old airfield – she pointed down a pock-marked strip of concrete. Did you see 'Heartbreak Ridge' with Clint Eastwood? About rescuing the medical students in Grenada?"

Mitch shook his head and looked blank.

"Well, we'll watch it tonight together. Most of that was filmed here. The scene where they're looking down at the hostiles is actually a line of residents getting on the ferry. The money the island made from that movie went to restore the lighthouse.

"Fun fact – the real U.S. military mission to Grenada actually did launch from Vieques. They staged on that airfield I pointed to back there, and then went to rescue the medical students from here," she said.

"That's cool!" Mitch agreed.

"You've probably seen Vieques beaches in lots of movies over the years. This was the only place that the U.S. military could practice bombing and assaulting a beach, and they used to let the movie studios film B-roll while it was happening to use in movies. Most of the movies filmed before 1999 that have a beach war scene with big ships contain some footage from those actual military exercises."

She took a tight right onto a dirt path off the gravel road and then another right down a steep driveway that ended in a small parking lot.

"Get out," Tally told Mitch with a grin. "We walk from here." Mitch carried the beach chairs and the umbrella and wore the lunch cooler on his back. Tally had their beach bag, towels, and the small cooler of drinks.

There was a fairly-steep gravel drive about 30 yards long that led down to the beach. Tally led Mitch around the chain meant to block vehicles. He followed her lead and stepped carefully down the path, and when they got to the bottom, she stopped to let him take it all in.

"Secret Beach," he said softly. "It's amazing."

Tally was excited to find there were only a few other people there, and they'd hiked to the far end of the beach to sit, almost a hundred yards away. Tally and Mitch walked down to the beach toward them a little way and set up their own chairs. Then she took him swimming.

"This is crazy," he said as they sat together in water up to their chins. Tally had been bouncing the sun off her engagement ring and giggling over the pretty prisms it created on the surface. "Does it ever get deep?"

"A little farther out it drops off. Then at the mouth of the bay it's suddenly ocean, so you don't want to go that far out. It's a popular snorkeling spot but you better have a life jacket and flippers."

They spent the entire day on the beach and in the water, and then went back to the hotel to nap before the biobay tour.

Chapter 21

It had been the perfect weekend in almost every way, Tally thought as they sat at Bananas, another popular restaurant, next door to Duffy's on the Malecon, eating dinner on Sunday evening. Their trip had flown by – they'd spent Saturday on Sun Bay and then went out to Red and Blue beaches on Sunday because they'd spent all of Friday at Secret Beach. As predicted, the beaches were packed and San Juanerros were blaring reggaeton as loud as they could from their boats at Caracas. Mitch found it hilarious – he loved people watching. Tally was much more relaxed in the afternoon when they settled themselves at a remote spot on Blue Beach. She'd been afraid of running into Eduardo or Anna Maria at Red.

The tour of Mosquito Bay on Saturday evening was magical. The clouds had obscured the moon and then at the end of the tour, it began to rain. Each rain drop turned into a splash of neon green as it struck the bioluminescent water. You couldn't take a picture of it with a regular camera so it was something Tally had really wanted Mitch to experience to understand.

The realtor had texted her earlier that everything was on target for the 2 p.m. closing on Monday afternoon at the Popular Mortgage office in Old San Juan. Tally planned to pack that night so they'd have time for one last breakfast at Hacienda Tamarindo before their flight. She didn't know when she would be back on Vieques but she suspected it would probably be a very long time.

After dinner, Tally and Mitch walked down the Malecon and stopped for a beer at Lazy Jack's. Tally had been avoiding the local hangout but she couldn't say no when the owners waved to her from across the street. She'd worked lot of welcome parties at his venue and he and his wife had always been good to her.

They took seats on stools at tables across from the bar with a view of the street and Tally introduced Mitch to the owners of Lazy Jack's. They chatted for a few minutes about how the island had changed – they already knew what Tally was up to via the coconut grapevine, which was usually more accurate than *The New York Times* – and then went behind the bar to help serve a rush of customers.

It was a pretty view of the Malecon but Tally couldn't relax. Knowing they were only two blocks away from Eduardo's parents' house, where she'd ridden out Hurricane Maria, was giving her a horrible, sick feeling, but she didn't want to tell Mitch about it and ruin their last evening. She declined when Mitch suggested getting them another beer, and told him they should get going instead since they had an early morning. Unfortunately, Tally was a few minutes too late.

"What the hell are you doing here?" a loud, female voice shrieked from behind them. Tally and Mitch both jerked around to see who was screaming.

"Oh damn," Tally said under her breath when she saw Eduardo's sister, Anna Maria, heading toward her from the other side of the bar. She quickly told Mitch, who had gotten off his stool and stood next to the table, who the woman was and what was happening.

"Let's just leave a tip for the waitress and get out of here," Tally whispered. "At this hour, she's probably drunk and I don't need to create a public spectacle."

"Understood." Mitch put a twenty-dollar bill on the table and took Tally's hand to leave.

"Where do you think you're going?" Anna Maria called to their backs as she tried to get through the pack of people blocking her path as they waited in line at the bar. Tally didn't acknowledge the woman she'd once thought would be her sister-in-law and, instead, picked up her pace. They'd left the car parked in the lot across at the other end of the Malecon and she hoped that Anna Maria wouldn't follow them. She'd watched the mean woman beat up more than one person at beach parties when she was dating Eduardo, and she didn't want to get hit. Mitch would never stand for her being attacked, and he would probably get arrested because Eduardo's family was connected to everybody on the island. Tally walked faster. Mitch kept up and didn't ask questions.

Nobody followed them to the Jeep, and Tally took the back road, Magnolia, around Esperanza instead of passing Lazy Jack's on their way back to Hacienda Tamarindo. She didn't say much on the car ride and Mitch kept her company in her silence.

When they got back to Room 5, Mitch opened the louvered French doors wide and poured them each a glass of champagne he'd kept stashed in their cooler for exactly this purpose. It was romantic and perfect. Just like being on the deck together in Jekyll, anywhere Tally was with Mitch, she was blissfully happy.

It was cool so they left the air-conditioning off and the windows open to let in the breeze. Mitch was already out cold when Tally heard sirens screaming in the night. It wasn't close by, but sound carried quite a distance on the 21-by-7-mile island. When she heard more sirens a moment later, she assumed it was probably a parade. It wasn't quite Christmas-time when, traditionally, random parrandas showed up on the neighbor's lawn in the middle of the night to blow everybody out of bed and play music until they were invited inside and fed. But there were too many sirens for it to be anything else so Tally went to sleep without giving it any more thought.

Chapter 22

Anna Maria saw red when she heard Tally was at Lazy Jack's. She'd hated that gringa when her brother was dating her and she'd hated her more after sharing space with her during the storm. They should have left Tally in the shack in Villa Borinquen, she thought, not for the first time. Letting her nemesis blow away in Hurricane Maria would have solved a lot of problems.

"How dare she come back here?" she asked her friend Nydia, who had kept her from going after Tally and the big gringo she had with her. "That was probably her boyfriend."

"No, *chica*," Nydia corrected her. "You didn't see the rock on her ring finger? They're engaged."

This information riled Anna Maria up even more. She'd been drinking with her friends for a couple of hours when she heard Tally was on the island and somewhere she could yell at her. She felt totally unsatisfied with the way things had ended. That little *puta* shouldn't have been able to walk away from her at Lazy Jack's scot-free after what she'd done to her older brother.

"Eduardo has been a mess since she left," Anna Maria muttered, putting all the blame for her brother's life failures on his ex-girlfriend. "He's still not working full-time."

Nydia knew otherwise. Eduardo wasn't working for the biobay full-time because he was working for one of the deeply embedded criminal organizations that made Vieques the biggest drug entry point in the United States. She knew this because her brother worked for the same gang and he'd mentioned Eduardo a few times when talking about business with her father. But it wasn't her place to try to change Anna Maria's mind. Besides, she liked watching her friend get fired up. Anna Maria was wild.

When she didn't get satisfaction by taking on Tally, Anna Maria decided she had a duty to tell Eduardo that the *bruja* was back, and with another man. She'd watched her older brother turn into an alcoholic with her father on their front steps in the months after the gringa abandoned him. At the worst time in a Viequenses' life, when the island had been ravaged, Tally had taken her privileged gringa ass back home and never given any of them another thought.

At first, Anna Maria had just been grateful to have her out of their house after Tally's Aunt Etah got her niece a flight off Vieques with a media transport, six weeks after the storm. Her mother had been outraged that Eduardo's girlfriend had left without looking back. But that hadn't stopped her from depositing the generous check Tally sent in a thank you note for her hospitality during and after the storm. The note on monogrammed stationery was just another snooty way of shoving her money in their faces, in Anna Maria's opinion.

But when Eduardo mourned Tally's departure in bottle after bottle of Palo Viejo – basically the cheapest way to stay drunk – Anna Maria didn't blame him for his behavior. She told her girlfriends who wanted to date Eduardo that all her brother needed was a good Puerto Rican woman to shake him out of his bad mood. But he wasn't friendly to the girls who flirted with him and had even been outright rude when Nydia got a little pushy one night. That pissed Anna Maria off even more. It was like that gringa had somehow ruined Eduardo forever. She wanted a little revenge.

She'd wanted Tally to leave Vieques, but she hadn't wanted her brother to be hurt. She was certain that the gringa could have stayed a while longer and helped Eduardo rebuild their casita. Instead, with her gone, he had no motivation to look for a job or move out of his parents' house. When Anna Maria suggested that she help him rebuild, and that they share the house, he hadn't even considered her offer. He'd just gone inside and refilled his drink, before going down the block to sit on a friend's porch away from her. It reminded her of how he'd stopped hanging out with her crowd and skipped their full moon parties after he started dating Tally. He'd wanted her to kiss the bitch's gringa ass and Anna Maria wasn't willing to do it, so the whiny girl had refused to participate in their social gatherings.

As far as she was concerned, her brother had been a fun, motivated guy until Tally had broken him, and to Anna Maria, that was unforgivable. It made her bitter. The nerve of that gringa to come back to their island with her new lover infuriated her. She wanted Eduardo to hit the guy.

She texted her brother and asked where he was. He replied that he was at Mar Azul, a bar on the other side of the island. Anna Maria thought about waiting to tell him about Tally until she saw him at home so she could see his reaction, but she couldn't help herself.

"That gringa you used to worship is back on the island," she wrote. "With her fiancé," she added in another text.

"Da fuq?" her brother replied, followed by a series of emojis meant to convey obscenities.

Anna Maria debated telling Eduardo that Tally and the guy had left. But that would deprive her of seeing her brother freak out. And that wouldn't be any fun.

"They're here at Lazy Jack's and she's dressed like a whore," she hit send without a second thought. She went to the bar to get another drink while she waited for the entertainment to begin.

It was about 15 minutes later when everyone at Lazy Jack's heard a "boom" and all of the lights in Esperanza went out. It wasn't an unusual occurrence to lose power and, initially, everybody assumed the sound had been a transformer blowing up. The military had built the power system on Vieques in the 1950s and the government of Puerto Rico never upgraded it so things went dark on all the time. Lazy Jack's kicked on their generator and a few minutes later, the bar was as if nothing had happened, even though most of the houses around them, and the streetlights, remained dark.

When police cars began racing through Esperanza, the locals on bar stools knew something more serious was going on. Nydia came back from the bar with a scoop.

"Somebody hit a power pole on Sun Bay road and the whole south side is dark," she reported.

Anna Maria finished her drink and sent a quick text to her brother, telling Eduardo not to get stuck behind the crash scene. Depending on how far across the island he'd gotten, he might have to turn around and go back to cut across. He didn't reply to her message but that wasn't unusual. Vehicles in Vieques weren't equipped with CarPlay or Bluetooth systems and you risked hitting a horse if you took your eyes off the road to read a message. So even her arrogant brother refrained from texting and driving.

Lazy Jack's got more crowded as people in dark houses emerged to find out why their air-conditioning had stopped. Duffy's and Bananas had shut down with the power, and the people who were at those bars drifted down the street to Lazy Jack's, drawn by the lights. The owners were making the most of the boon – offering $1 shots of cheap booze passed on trays by their pretty waitresses. Nobody cared when they stayed open after legal closing time because every cop on the island was at the crash scene.

Anna Maria was having a pretty good time with her friends – it felt like a hurricane party – when her mother ran into the bar in her nightgown, screaming hysterically. She couldn't understand her at first but then it clicked and everything in Anna Maria's world started spinning.

Chapter 23

Tally and Mitch went up to breakfast when it started at 7 a.m. They were ready to check out and return the rental car so they could catch their flight at 9.

"Don't take Sun Bay road across the island," the friendly girl behind the front desk warned when Tally handed in their keys. "There was a really bad accident there late last night and they're still waiting for the medical examiner to arrive."

"Thanks for the heads up. We had a great time here." She slid a cash tip to the girl before she left.

She relayed the information about the wreck to Mitch when she climbed into the Jeep. He'd already loaded everything and was backed in, waiting for her.

"We'll go through Esperanza but then take a left on the Cross-Island Expressway instead of taking the road past Camp Garcia," she told him. Most people wouldn't have mapped the island in their head in just a few days, but Mitch was a cop and his brain worked differently. She knew he understood what she was talking about.

"Cross-Island Expressway – actually it's Rt. 996 – but you'll get why we call it that when you see it. It's the closest thing to a highway on this island. Sometimes you can even go 45," she joked.

They drove through Esperanza and Tally told Mitch how she'd loved morning meetings on the Malecon because of the way the water sparkled. He saw what she meant. Jekyll was beautiful but the water there wasn't blue.

There was no sign of the accident until after Tally rounded the bend by the Green Store. The state police actually had Rt. 997 – otherwise known as Sun Bay Road – blocked off at the Cross-Island Expressway. An officer standing next to his motorcycle, with his helmet on, waved their Jeep toward the detour.

"If the crash was last night, why is the road still closed?" Mitch asked as they made the turn.

"Somebody died in the wreck, according to the desk clerk."

"What does that have to do with it?" His trooper brain was thinking even the worst investigators could clear a single-vehicle crash scene in less than eight hours.

"They can't move the body until the medical examiner says so," she explained.

"Right, same as us," Mitch nodded. It wasn't adding up for him.

"But the medical examiner is based on the big island. Probably coming from San Juan. And whoever drew the short straw and had to cover Vieques and Culebra this weekend obviously didn't feel like taking the first ferry."

Mitch looked at Tally with disbelief.

"Seriously," Tally continued. "I wasn't here when this happened, but Isabelle tells a story about a kid who was murdered in a drug war on that corner across from Green Store – in the big empty lot with the old train skeleton we just passed – on Christmas Eve. But nobody from the medical examiner's office came to Vieques until the morning of the 26th. That kid's body sat out there on the ground, in the sun, under a sheet through all of Christmas Day with people driving by him and the cop left there to watch the scene."

"Oh my God."

"Isabelle said his family sat by his body the whole time, just outside the tape, in beach chairs," she recalled, cringing visibly. "This is part of the United States, but Vieques is more like a Third World country in many aspects. You heard those loudspeaker trucks blasting through the neighborhoods? That's the only source of local news here. Vieques and its sister island, Culebra, are the very last places the feds or Puerto Rican government help when there is a natural disaster."

Tally paid JoJo in cash when they dropped off the car, and the friendly guy drove the couple to the airport so they wouldn't have to wait for a taxi. It cracked Mitch up that all they had to do to check in for their flight was stop at a makeshift counter and barely show ID. One of the guys at the gate recognized Tally and chatted with her briefly in Spanish and suddenly nobody cared about checking their documents. He had his license in his hand but nobody ever asked to see it, so he put it back in his pocket when he saw them printing out baggage tags.

The Vieques Airlink plane was a lot older than the one Cape Air had flown them over to the island on, and Mitch was skeptical when they climbed into their assigned seats on the fully-booked 35-year-old Cessna Caravan. They were allowed to keep their carry-ons with them on this flight, and they got to sit next to each other. Tally rolled her eyes at Mitch, who was perplexed by the different policies. Her state trooper fiancé would not love living in the Caribbean. He saw everything in black and white. Puerto Ricans existed in a constantly-changing shade of gray.

The pilot did a full circle over Old San Juan as he lined up for the runway at Isla Grande, and Mitch and Tally were both mesmerized by the view. She pointed out the fort they were going to go see and the governor's mansion, La Fortaleza. After they made a bumpy landing – due to the condition of the runway, not the pilot – they jumped into a taxi waiting outside the little airport and asked the driver to take them to El Convento.

The plan was to get checked into their hotel and dump their luggage. She wanted to have an early lunch with Mitch in the lovely café in the park inside El Convento. Depending on how much time they had before the scheduled 2 p.m. closing, they might be able to tour the cathedral across the street before they needed to go to the mortgage company.

Tally watched Mitch take in the narrow, cobbled streets and the daredevil drivers as their taxi made its way from the port area up to El Convento.

"See why I didn't want to rent a car over here?" she asked.

"I gotcha now."

"Uh huh," she replied with a smirk.

Mitch had wanted to rent a Jeep on the big island so they could go explore the El Yunque rainforest one of the days they were there. Tally had put her foot down and told him they'd come back to Puerto Rico again and visit El Yunque on another trip, neither of them could drive in Old San Juan. The streets were so narrow in places – with cars parked on both sides of the road – that they both held their breath repeatedly as their taxi squeezed through.

She could tell her fiancé felt relieved when the taxi stopped in front of a uniformed bellman outside El Convento. "Feel more like the real world?" she asked.

"Not sure it feels real," he admitted. "But it's a lot of fun seeing all of this with you and hearing about living here through your eyes."

"I didn't spend that much time over here on the big island," Tally said. "Mostly, I was in and out for shopping trips. But the few times I stayed in San Juan, I stayed here."

The hotel check-in was located on an upper floor of the hotel, with a view of the courtyard below. Their room was ready when they arrived, even though it wasn't yet noon. So, they got the keys and followed the bellman and his loaded cart up to a suite on the top floor.

"I think we got upgraded because it's a Monday," she explained. "There's nobody here on weekdays unless they have meetings at La Fortaleza." The governor's mansion a few blocks away was like the White House of Puerto Rico.

They were unpacking their suitcases when Tally's phone rang. She'd turned it on and meant to check voicemails in the car, but totally forgot. She was more relaxed than she'd been in a very long time and she knew that she'd get a 911 text from one of the girls if things went sideways back home. She was on the opposite side of the room taking things out of their hanging bag so Mitch picked up the ringing phone on the dresser and read the display.

"Yaya," he announced.

"Ooo, answer that," Tally grunted as she heaved clothing onto the rack. "I want to talk to her."

"Hey Yaya, hang on a sec for Tally," he answered her phone and then walked over to hand it to her.

"Thanks," she told him. "Hola Chiquita! I'm in Puerto Rico and you're not, how weird is that?"

"So weird," Yaya agreed, but she wasn't laughing like Tally. "Where are you guys?"

"Just checked into El Convento. We're getting unpacked. Closing is at 2 p.m."

"Put the phone on speaker and sit down," Yaya told her. Tally did as she was instructed, setting the phone on the bed. Mitch looked at her with a curious expression.

"Are you sitting down?" Yaya asked.

"Yes," Tally flopped on the big bed dramatically. "What's going on? Did we get fired by a client?"

"Oh God no, this has nothing to do with Jekyll Island."

"Thank God," Tally felt a little guilty to feel relieved. "And Etah is okay?"

"Your aunt is fine. But Tally, I thought you would want to know... Eduardo was killed in a car crash last night on Sun Bay Road."

Tally's jaw dropped and she said nothing. She was stunned. Mitch picked up her pink iPhone and turned off the speaker. He spoke quietly to Yaya as he paced the room, getting details that Tally would want to hear later but couldn't handle at that moment. Tally wanted to protest – to scream TELL ME WHAT'S GOING ON – but she couldn't find it in her. She was just spent. Everything went out of her in a whoosh.

"You want to talk to Tally?" she heard Mitch ask Yaya.

"I want to talk to her," Tally called, and he brought her the phone.

"Sorry," she told her best friend. "That hit me weird. I can't believe he's gone. And I doubly can't believe I was on the island when it happened, and we left without knowing. Not that his parents would have wanted to see me anyway, I don't know what I'm thinking. It's just strange knowing we were there. I have to process this."

"Me, too," Yaya agreed. "I went to school with him, remember? I didn't like him but I've known him forever. I guess I thought he was one of those guys that would always be there when I went back to visit, whether I wanted to see him or not. That sounds bad."

"No, I get what you're saying. I wonder what happened."

"He was speeding and he lost control – probably to avoid a horse, the police think – and smashed into an electric pole. The car caught fire and there was a big-ass boom and all the power on the south side of the island went out. You probably didn't even notice because Hacienda Tamarindo has a generator bigger than a truck that kicks on automatically," she reminded her.

"He always drove too fast on that road," Tally said softly.

"Everybody does. Til they have a close encounter of the equine kind."

"That didn't stop Eduardo," Tally protested. "He was so hard-headed."

She thanked Yaya for giving her the news. They discussed whether Tally should go to the funeral or send something, and decided it was best to let sleeping dogs lie. She hadn't seen Eduardo or his parents while she was in Vieques, and the hostile encounter with Anna Maria at Lazy Jack's didn't make her think she'd be welcome to pay her respects. She told Yaya about it.

"Tally, you don't want to be there. You broke up three years ago, and if you didn't happen to be there now, you wouldn't even consider going back for his funeral. Take my advice and just let it go. Anna Maria is a beast, and you know it. If you cross her path, she's going to come after you and everybody will say it's 'just fine' because she's grieving."

Yaya wasn't kidding. Tally remembered attending the funeral of a friend's mother in the "new" cemetery on the little island. Some of the coffins buried in the "old" cemetery had slid into the ocean during Hurricane Hugo in 1989 so everybody who died after that was buried a few miles up the road, a little bit further from the edge of the water. The cemetery was rustic, to say the least. There was one concrete area with a permanent bier in the middle to hold the guest of honor during a service. Then the casket and flowers were loaded into funeral vehicles – circa 1950 Cadillacs – and driven across the cemetery to the pre-dug hole. It was easy to find the grave because there was a piece of construction equipment parked next to it. Tally's jaw had dropped when her friend's father had thrown himself across his dead wife's casket during the service, sobbing and beating his chest. His older sister followed suit and the cacophony of grief blew Tally's mind. She'd only seen that sort of behavior in movies. And she'd been to a lot of funerals in her life.

"You're right," she told Yaya. "I'm not thinking straight. We're going to get this closing over with today and enjoy San Juan tomorrow and then come home."

"Good. Because we need you back here. I've picked up so many new flower clients for this spring that it's crazy. I wanted to know where we should cap it during the time we blocked off for your wedding. We can still do flowers for other weddings during that, right?"

"Sure," Tally agreed. "But not after Thursday of my wedding week. If it can't be delivered to them by noon on Thursday, we should refer them to somebody else. We're going to have enough to do with my flowers and I want you and Kayla to be able to have fun at my wedding, too. No more work than you absolutely, positively have to do to make my wedding perfect," she joked.

Her mood was improving as she thought about the future, and she ended the call after asking Yaya to give Kayla her love. She went into the bathroom and looked in the mirror. She was still herself. But something inside her felt like everything had changed. She hadn't wanted to ever see Eduardo again, but she'd hoped he'd have a happy and full life.

Mitch knocked on the bathroom door. "You okay, babe?"

She opened the bathroom door and smiled at him. "Yeah, I'm fine. It's just a shock. Not the kind of news you can ever expect to get. He was the first guy I ever fell in love with."

"Aw, Tally," Mitch wrapped his arms around the woman he loved and pulled her onto his lap on the bed. She finally let the tears go.

Chapter 24

The rest of their Puerto Rican adventure had gone by in a blur. The closing on Isabelle's villa went fine, but it took more than five hours to complete the paperwork. They'd had to catch a taxi directly from Popular Mortgage over to the famous Parrot Club, where Tally had secured reservations. Dinner was great but there was a pall over the night. She didn't want to go dancing at the local clubs afterwards like she'd thought they would do when she made their reservations. She hadn't gotten to put on her sexy outfit or her dancing shoes before dinner anyway.

The next day, Tally showed Mitch El Morro and after taking obligatory pictures all over the historic fort, they went for ice cream and strolled through Old San Juan to shop for gifts to bring back for their family and friends. Tally was relieved when the plane took off the next morning with them on it. She was ready to go home and wasn't sure she'd ever be back. There were lots of beautiful places in the Caribbean that didn't hold such dark memories for her.

***

Tally and Mitch both hit the ground running after they got home. He had to work on his days off for a couple weeks to pay back guys who had swapped with him, and she had a pile of potential clients to work through, plus wedding plans to make for them. They'd talked about wedding details on the flight home – it was a happy topic and distracted her from the sad news she was still processing. She needed to stay focused on their future and leave the past behind her in Vieques, where it belonged.

She told Mitch she didn't want to use the "same old formula" for their wedding that she used to plan all of her clients' events.

"What formula?" he asked.

"Welcome party, beach or pool party, wedding, farewell brunch," Tally rattled off.

"But isn't that what works best for you on a consistent basis? Why would you change it and risk chaos at our wedding? I don't get it," Mitch said with a frown.

"I just want it to be different," she insisted. She wasn't able to articulate what she was thinking so they let that subject go and moved on to discussing music.

She had the same conversation with Isabelle and Yaya a few nights later. Yaya had come over for a girls' night while Mitch was out working, and they'd done a virtual call with Isabelle. She'd just been released from the rehab facility and had therapists coming by her house on a daily basis to continue to help her regain her footing. She showed the girls how she was doing with her walking via the webcam.

"Sit down, you're making me nervous," Tally ordered her friend. "Don't need you to break the other hip."

"Oh poo," Isabelle argued, but she did return to her seat and flop into the chair. "I'm fine. I got hurt because I slipped on ice and that has nothing to do with my age. I could have broken my wrist or cracked my noggin – I didn't break my hip because I'm old. I did it because I'm a klutz."

"Uh huh," Yaya muttered. "You never slipped on ice in Vieques." Tally looked at her and they both cracked up.

"Very funny, girls. Very funny," Isabelle chuckled too. "But back to the topic at hand – Tally's wedding."

"I don't want to talk about my wedding anymore," Tally whined. "And my drink is empty."

"So is mine," Yaya complained.

"I shall solve this crisis," Tally announced and jumped up from the table where they'd been sitting in front of a laptop. Isabelle could see hands snatch their empty beverage glasses and then heard Tally talking to herself as she mixed drinks.

"So tell me the details on Eduardo's crash," Isabelle whispered to Yaya while Tally was distracted.

"Oh, it's nasty. One of my friends dates a guy that works for the electric company, and she texted me a picture he sent her of what was left of Eduardo when *los bomberos* finally got the fire out. You wanna see it?"

"You tell me. Do I want to see it?"

"Probably not," Yaya decided. "All that's left of him looked like a fried turkey."

"What looked like a fried turkey?" Tally yelled and then re-entered the screen. She plopped one glass in front of Yaya and kept the other. "I don't remember whose was whose." She took a long sip.

"Yours was the pink straw," Yaya told her, shaking her head. "You always get the pink straw. Why do you keep forgetting that?"

Tally shrugged and laughed. Then switched their glasses.

"What were you two talking about behind my back? I heard you whispering. I don't want any surprises at my wedding. You know the rules." She laughed as she said it but the women knew she was not joking. More than once, Tally had put the kibosh on surprising a bride the night before her wedding or even on the day of.

"We wouldn't dare," Yaya promised. "We know better than that."

"We were talking about Eduardo," Isabelle admitted. Yaya glared at her through the video screen and the older woman shrugged.

"What about Eduardo?" Tally asked.

"Just that authorities couldn't determine whether alcohol played a factor in the crash because there wasn't enough left of him to test after the fire," Yaya told her, leaving out the part about the picture of his remains looking like fried turkey carcass. She'd loved the guy, after all. "The bartender told cops that he'd been drinking shots with Davio most of the night."

"It was after midnight and he was speeding on Sun Bay Road," Tally said. "Of course, alcohol was a factor. It was always a factor for him after 5 p.m., and from what I've heard about him since I left, he started drinking even earlier after the storm. Oof," she sighed. "This has got to be so hard for his family. I wonder who I would call to send his mother flowers now that Vieques Flowers is gone."

"I'll get you a number," Yaya promised. "But think hard about what you want to say on the card. His family is nuts and Anna Maria really hated you."

"Thanks for the reminder. It's not like it was my fault. I didn't even see him while I was there. I barely saw Anna Maria. She mostly just saw my backside as we ran for the car."

"Yeah, but think about whether you sending flowers will be received in the way that you mean it. Or if it will come across the wrong way to grieving people who already have a grudge against you," Isabelle suggested. "If you're doing it for them, fine. If you're doing it to make yourself feel better, don't. You don't want to do more damage than good with best intentions."

Tally agreed to think on it some more before she sent anything to anyone in Eduardo's family. Yaya reported that the funeral had been a traditional, huge Viequenses affair. His family and friends had filled the sidewalk and street overnight on the night before he was to be buried. They stood drinking Coors Light they'd brought in coolers and cups of hot chocolate from a dispenser at the only funeral home on the island. He'd been buried in the new cemetery and his cousins had lowered the casket into the ground before the piece of heavy equipment staged next to it shoveled dirt on top of the box.

Yaya reported that her sister's boyfriend's mom had seen Anna Maria screaming and yelling hysterically at the grave site.

"Even more over the top than what you've seen. Gina said that she thought she was going to jump in the hole on the flowers, but her boyfriend held her back."

Yaya left out that Anna Maria had reportedly screamed threats about Tally, and promised vengeance for her older brother's death, because she wanted to talk to Isabelle about it separately first. She was pretty sure Anna Maria's threats of "Viequenses justice" wouldn't translate to problems in Georgia, and Tally had enough going on in her head with wedding groups on the island and her own wedding to plan.

Isabelle promised to check in daily with the girls and keep them posted on her recovery progress. They promised to rush to her aid if she needed them, but she laughed and told them, again, that she was fine on her own.

Chapter 25

The holidays flew by that year, with Tally orchestrating high-dollar Christmas parties for residents and businesses on the island. Jekyll Flowers was supplying holiday arrangements and décor to multiple hotels on the island. Her business didn't book weddings over the holidays, as a rule, but Yaya had wanted to work through Christmas. She was a businesswoman, and she knew darned well how much she could make during that time of year on Jekyll, while thousands of tourists were visiting the island to see the Holly Jolly Jekyll light display that had won so many big awards. Tally insisted she received a "holiday rate" for her pay in December that would include a percentage of the shop's overall sales.

"It's only fair since you're doing all the work. And just because you do it this year, doesn't mean you have to do it next year," Tally was hoping Yaya would stay in Georgia forever and she didn't want her friend to feel trapped at the shop. Yaya saw it as an opportunity to bank money towards eventually buying her own place in the area.

Kayla had opted to go home to Iowa and visit family over the holidays, and Tally had surprised her by bumping her ticket up to first class with credit card points. Yaya and Kayla were the reason she was able to run these businesses and she wanted them to feel appreciated.

Mitch had to work a lot but he'd had off on all of the major holidays, which his mother loved and his father teased him about. When Tally had to work a party on New Year's Eve, he tagged along as her assistant so they could be together when the clock struck midnight.

***

Engagement season hit them full force before Valentine's Day, with all the brides who'd gotten engaged over the holidays arriving on the island for venue tours. The flower shop was swamped and Yaya had to hire extra help to get all of the Valentine's Day orders delivered exactly when requested. Kayla and Tally were too busy with wedding clients to be of much help. It was a holy nightmare and total chaos in the shop, but Yaya thrived on it.

Tally worked from home most of those days unless her hands were needed to murder roses. It turned out that a surprising number of customers would pay $75 for a sandwich bag of flawless rose petals to sprinkle on their beds or wherever. Yaya recommended two bags to make a heart on the bedspread and people were actually taking her advice. It was madness, and her friend had taken to leaving buckets of roses at Tally's house for her to murder in front of the TV for the past three nights. When she was done, Mitch would take the finished bags of petals – not zipped shut so they didn't rot – back to the shop later that night and pop them in the fridge so Yaya would have them in the morning. So far, they'd sold out three days in a row.

Tally needed to do her own wedding chores after work, too. Cheryl came over one night when Mitch was on duty to help Tally stuff and address their wedding invitations.

"Ya know, my mother always flips over the invitation to see if it's engraved or not before she looks to see who is getting married," Cheryl told Tally. Her mother was an old-school southern lady and this information didn't surprise Tally at all.

"I'm going to flunk her test," she said. "I used regular thermography."

"Oh, that's okay, one day I'll disappoint her too. I'm not going to spend an extra few thousand dollars so that my mother can feel snotty," Cheryl declared.

"Wanna bet?" Tally asked with a smile.

"No. I hate you," her friend joked. "She's probably already got it drafted out for the engraving plates – she just needs a name of a groom."

"Probably," Tally agreed.

Etah had volunteered to be the hostess for the wedding, as far as the invitations were concerned. Tally had played with it, but ultimately decided to make the invitation from her and Mitch, rather than their parents, since hers had been gone so long. Tally had run it by Bonnie and Roberta to make sure there wouldn't be any hurt feelings, and both women assured her that they wanted her to do it whatever way made her most comfortable.

It was a bit of a touchy subject. The mother of the bride was usually a character that the wedding planners joked about – she'd either be awesome or awful, and there weren't many in between. Tally had learned that the hard way. But it didn't make her miss her mom any less when vendors who didn't know her life story asked if her mother would be joining them for the cake tasting and dress fittings. She felt like she'd had to explain that her parents were dead more times during her wedding planning than she had in her whole life.

Tally had struggled to find the right dress. She'd seen literally every design on every shape of bride and knew what she absolutely, positively did not want to wear. But she didn't find many that didn't have some element she considered a fatal flaw. For example, she didn't want to wear lace, but she thought she'd be miserably hot in silk satin. She wanted a train on the dress but she didn't want a French bustle because they were pain in the ass. She and Yaya actually got in an argument about whether Tally would wear heels on her wedding day. As a general rule, she hated them.

"You are not going to have ugly-ass flats in your wedding pictures," Yaya insisted. "You don't have to wear them all night – you can take them off after the first dance."

"Gee thanks, that's nice of you," Tally had snarked. "Maybe I'll just dance barefoot."

Yaya looked horrified. Puerto Ricans, as a general rule, were much more formal at their weddings than gringos. For example, nobody born on a Caribbean island wanted to have an outdoor wedding there. Only gringos wanted to sweat at their destination weddings. The locals who worked the Vieques Weddings events had always joked about "crazy gringos" as they doused themselves in bug repellant and fanned themselves before the receptions.

"You're not dancing barefoot, we'll find you some heels you don't hate," Yaya put a period on the argument with a tone that Tally dared not challenge. They looked at each other and started laughing.

"Shut up," Tally giggled. "You're going to be the same pain in the ass when you get married."

"I won't be as bad as you."

Chapter 26

Most of Tally's spring weddings went smoothly. Every wedding had a hiccup of one form or the other. Either a vendor had a problem or a guest behaved badly – the snafu would be one side or the other, rarely both at the same wedding. But no matter what had caused a problem, it was up to Tally and Kayla to triage the situation before their brides and grooms ever became aware of it. And they were pretty good at their jobs.

There'd been a near disaster at the Yardley/Cotter wedding when the bride's cousin, fresh out of rehab, had taken all of the methadone she'd been given for the entire trip on the first night. She'd freaked out and left the island with her sketchy boyfriend and they were allegedly holed up in a hotel in Savannah with a pile of drugs.

Good riddance, Tally had thought when she'd heard the news at breakfast the next morning. But the bride was in full meltdown by the time she saw Tally at her bridesmaids' luncheon on the pool deck at the Jekyll Island Club Hotel.

Through hysterical tears, the bride explained that her "stupid druggy cousin" had taken her bridesmaid dress with her when she made her getaway.

"I always wanted Melissa to be a bridesmaid, but my mother made me ask Sarah because all my other girl cousins are in the wedding and it would seem mean. And it's super important to me that in pictures we have the exact same number of attendants on each side," she cried to Tally, who handed her a tissue from her purse. "I hate uneven wedding parties."

"Blow your nose and take a deep breath," Tally told her calmly, a benevolent smile on her face.

"But but but…" the bride started weeping again. "Melissa is the same size as Sarah and so she can wear the dress and we'll have even numbers. But Sarah took the dress with her even though my mom paid for it." There was righteous indignation in her wobbly voice.

"Oh my God," Tally agreed, sounding horrified. "That is so rude. I cannot even. Listen, honey. Don't you dare let this take up one more second of space in your head today. Go fix your face before the guests start arriving so this doesn't become the hot topic of the day, and I'll get the dress back before the wedding."

The tears stopped instantly. "Really?"

"Really," Tally promised. "Just text me her info and where you think she's staying right now. This might cost a little bit because somebody is going to have to run to wherever she is to get it, I'd imagine."

"That's fine," the mother of the bride interjected, sounding a little desperate. "Just get the dress."

Kayla kept the trains running on time for the rest of the day while Tally left to try and keep her promise to the bride. Tally went out to her car and tried to call Sarah, the dress-stealing cousin, at the number she'd been given. Nobody answered and she left a nice voicemail asking the bride's cousin to call her back so she could arrange to pick up the bridesmaid dress. She hadn't thought to get the skeevy boyfriend's name, but she was pretty sure they had it on the guest list and placecard chart back at the office.

She went to the flower shop and Yaya helped her find the guy's name. Then Tally called the hotel where they thought they were staying and asked if there was anyone by the cousin or the boyfriend's name. There was, and Tally asked to be connected. A young female voice answered on the second ring.

"Hi Sarah, this is Tally the wedding planner," she started super friendly. "I understand that you decided not to be in the wedding. That's your prerogative, but you took your bridesmaid's dress with you when you left Jekyll. Your cousin would like to have it back so that one of the other girls can wear it."

"But it's my dress!" Sarah blurted. "Mine!"

"I guess so," Tally wasn't going to argue technicalities with a woman who used her drug-rehab medication recreationally.

"But the nice thing to do here would be to let her have the dress back," Tally said gently. "If you paid for it, I'm sure she'd reimburse you." That was Tally's tactful way of pointing out Sarah hadn't paid for the dress she was holding hostage. "She's kind of obsessed about having the exact same number of attendants on each side, and we don't want her to have to fire a groomsman. That's not fair to the groom."

"I'm not interested," the girl on the other end of the phone said. "I heard them talking about me at the welcome party – nobody wants me there. They're all glad my parents are dead." Tally might have felt terribly sorry for this girl crying on the other end of the phone if the bride's mother hadn't already blamed her sister's death on stress caused by her drug-addicted daughter.

"Oh Sarah, nobody is glad about that. I'm so sorry you misheard something and thought that." For one second, Tally considered whether she should try to get the girl to return to Jekyll for the wedding, but she thought better of it.

"Look, I can have somebody come up there and pick up the dress right now," Tally said, having no idea who was available to go. She'd figure that out next. "Can you just take it down to the front desk in the dress bag and leave it there with my name on it? Get it out of there so you don't have to think about all of this." She asked the question sweetly, as if she agreed with Sarah that this was all terribly unfair.

Methadone cousin didn't buy it. "Nope. Tell my cousin that her friends shouldn't have been bitches to me and tell Melissa she's too fat for my dress anyway." Then she hung up the phone with a satisfying slam that can only be had nowadays on a real land-line phone like the one in a hotel room.

Tally had put her phone on speaker about halfway through the rant so Yaya could be entertained, too. After she hung up, Yaya offered to go get the dress.

"I have some pent-up aggression I could relieve on that little twit," she explained.

Tally laughed and declined her kind offer. "I need you to finish flowers for the weddings; I'm going to sic Jekyll Errand Girl on this if I can confirm the dress is at the desk. They can do the running and we'll bill it to the MOB," she said, referring to the acronym they used for mother of the bride on all their paperwork and schedules.

Mitch called just then, and Tally ranted to him about the stupid mission that was wasting her precious time.

"Do you really think they have drugs in the hotel room?" he asked.

"I don't know. Probably. That's not the frigging point of this story, Mitch. The point is the dress," she used a tone that implied "duh."

"I get that, Tally. But if the guy you keep calling 'skeevy' hears that a trooper is on his way to get the dress, he might be more willing to run downstairs and leave it at the desk, don't you think? How old is the cousin?"

"Not old enough. But you can't go up there, can you?" She was utterly confused.

"No, I'm not going to Savannah to get the dress, unless you don't have anybody else to do it. But I'm telling you. Just tell him that you're sending your state trooper future husband to get the dress and see what happens."

"Okay," she still didn't sound convinced.

"You really need more practice at this cop-wife stuff," he joked.

"I'm not a cop wife yet," she shot back. "But I guess I need to hang out with Robin and her friends more."

"That would work. Let me know what happens and if you need me to go get that dress. I love you," Mitch said goodbye and hung up.

Tally looked at Yaya and shrugged; then she tried to call Sarah back. First on her cell phone and then through the hotel's front desk. Nobody answered in the room this time.

"Text her," Yaya suggested. "She's probably reading them even if she doesn't reply."

"Maybe," Tally allowed, and started tapping out a message.

"You should scare the shit out of her," Yaya said.

"Okay, tell me what you think," Tally began reading, "*Hi Sarah, I don't want to get ugly about this, but if the dress isn't waiting at the front desk of the hotel within an hour, I will send my state trooper boyfriend to your room to get it.* Do you think that sounds like a threat?"

"Not to a normal person," Yaya said. "To somebody sitting in a hotel room full of drugs it might be taken differently, but that's not on you. Hit send."

Tally did, and they got a response back faster than expected. Sarah said she was taking the dress down to the desk, immediately.

"Text me to confirm when it's down there," she texted back. Then she and Yaya exchange fist bumps and high fives.

When she got that confirmation text from Sarah a few minutes later, she called the hotel and asked if the dress had been left at the desk. After confirming it was there and asking the desk manager to hide it, she called Jamie, the owner of Jekyll Errand Girl, and asked if she could have somebody pick it up that same day. Jamie's husband was a retired law enforcement officer and her business slogan was, "If it's not illegal, we can probably do it." Her company literally provided every service imaginable, from elder care to airport transportation.

Jamie confirmed that she could have the dress picked up within a couple of hours and Tally happily gave her the bride's mother's credit card numbers.

"Thank you so much for doing this last minute," Tally told her. "You're saving my butt."

"That's what we do," Jamie said. "But later when you have time, I want to hear the whole backstory to this one. Sounds good." The women laughed and Tally thanked her and said goodbye.

She sent a quick text to Kayla with an update, and Kayla sent back a happy picture of the bride giving a thumbs up at the news. She forwarded the picture to Jamie with the caption, "another happy client! Couldn't have done it without you. Thanks again."

Not every wedding hiccup could be fixed as smoothly as the druggy-cousin's bridesmaid dress caper, unfortunately. Another spring wedding had been going smoothly all weekend until the bride stepped on her own wedding gown during the reception and went ass-over-tea kettle down the steps of her reception venue. Tally had seen her fall. She was a really big girl and she landed hard a couple of steps down, cracking her head on the stone staircase in the process. Tally heard it hit. But it didn't stop there. The bride bounced and rolled down another step and smacked her head again before she landed in a heap at the bottom.

"Call an ambulance," Tally told Kayla as she rushed to the fallen bride's side. The bride was out cold, but Tally didn't see blood. The groom was one second behind her and much calmer than his wedding planner.

"She does this all the time," he told Tally, pulling smelling salts out of his jacket pocket. He broke the package and waved it under his new bride's nose. After a few seconds, she came to and opened her eyes.

The groom would have been happy to get his still-dizzy bride up and dancing after that, but Tally insisted that the paramedics take her to the hospital to have her head examined by a doctor. It wasn't bleeding, but there was a huge divot in her head next to a growing bump. She couldn't risk that the bride had a brain bleed or some other injury they couldn't see and maybe go to bed and not wake up after her wedding.

The groom rode in the ambulance with the woman he'd been married to for just over four hours, and Tally followed in their rental car. She'd left Kayla to shut things down at the wedding – people were already departing the venue before the ambulance arrived – and told her to leave the cake set up so they could cut it in the morning. She called Mitch, who was off-duty and home, to tell him what was going on. She asked him to meet her at the hospital to give her a ride back to the venue afterwards.

"I'm just going to go in and make sure she's doing okay and give him the car keys so they can get home when she's released, if she's released," she explained.

"No problem. I'll be there to pick you up. Need anything else?"

"Just a massage when I get home," she told him. "I'm crazy stiff. I've never had a bride just drop on me before. Scared the crap out of me," she admitted. "She was out for at least a minute. She really smacked her head."

"And her husband said it happens all the time?"

"Yep, first thing he said," Tally reported.

"That's so weird."

"Yeah, I'm not sure that I want to know details on that," she chuckled.

It wasn't the first time Mitch had gotten dressed to go help Tally late at night. He'd showed up without her even calling him for help on a night when he was home listening to the scanner and heard a call for the address where his fiancée was orchestrating an event. He heard the dispatcher say "fight" and was out the door in a flash. He called Tally from his truck as he drove way too fast along Beachview, but she didn't answer. That scared him because she almost always answered his calls. Even during a wedding.

He arrived at the wedding venue at the same time as the state trooper who was actually on-duty on Jekyll that night. They shook hands and Mitch explained why he was there, and then he backed the guy up as they went into the multi-million-dollar mansion where the reception was being held.

Nobody answered their knock on the door, but they could hear a male voice yelling inside. The door was unlocked, so they let themselves in and went towards the melee. Mitch found Tally standing, with her arms folded, in front of a frantic catering staff who appeared to be packing up as fast as they could. A man continued yelling at her until he noticed the men in the doorway, one of them in a uniform.

Tally made eye contact with Mitch and he winked at her.

"What's going on?" the other trooper asked.

While that trooper talked to the drunk jerk who'd been screaming at his fiancé, Mitch got the scoop from Tally and Kayla. The jerk was the bride's brother and he was staying at the house. He'd accused the wedding staff of having stolen all of the cash out of his wallet during the reception held downstairs.

"Any chance that's true?" he asked Tally.

"Sure, there's a chance, but it's highly unlikely. The bride and groom are both military police officers and the staff know that. If nobody has ever taken anything before, at any of our weddings, why would they suddenly do it during a cop wedding? That doesn't even make sense. Everybody here has worked for us before, multiple times," she said.

"I agree. But MPs are different from regular cops," Mitch said, fulfilling a negative stereotype about trooper's opinions of other law enforcement branches. "No respectable LEO should let a family member treat an employee like he was berating you."

"Well, he wanted to search the catering staff and I was standing between them and him. I don't need him to like me tomorrow, but I need the caterers to be willing to work for future clients. And this guy was getting scary with his threats."

The caterers finished packing up and were quietly loading their cars under Mitch's watchful eye. The trooper, sick of the drunk guy's ranting, asked the "victim" to show him where the money was stolen. He came back down the stairs with the bride's unapologetic brother behind him a few minutes later. The money had fallen out of his pants when he dropped them on the floor. The wad of cash had been clearly visible, he'd just been too drunk to find it. And no, nobody apologized to the staff he'd mistreated.

Most of her weddings only suffered little blips, like a broken bustle on a wedding gown that Tally could fix with one of the massive diaper pins she kept in the bridal emergency bag for just such a purpose. Super-drunk guests were a problem every so often, but most of them got the message when she suggested it was time to go home and cut them off at the bar. Almost every wedding had an Aunt Mary and an Uncle Charlie, and if nothing else went wrong, those characters would keep it interesting.

"Aunt Mary" was always the wedding guest who thought she should have planned the wedding. She'd ask the wedding planning team nosy questions and repeatedly suggest they should be doing something – like toasts or cutting the cake – when she thought it was the right time, never mind the bride's schedule. She was pushy and bossy and staff made an effort to rescue each other if they saw somebody trapped in her clutches. Aunt Mary wanted to be in charge.

"Uncle Charlie" was the drunk uncle who groped the female staff at every wedding. He was a friendly guy who cozied up to the wedding planners at the welcome party because his own family avoided him. Tally and Kayla could usually spot Uncle Charlie on the first night, and they would warn each other - and the girls working the events - to avoid getting too close.

So far, they'd managed to handle all of the Uncle Charlies in a calm manner, but someday Uncle Charlie was going to get slapped across the face by somebody on her payroll (maybe even her) and Tally was okay with that.

The staff used Aunt Mary and Uncle Charlie as code names to deal with those particular wedding guests and most of the time it worked pretty well. They had other code names they made up on the fly – most of them less-than-flattering – so they could chat about people on their headsets without worrying about being overheard. It wasn't nice, Tally knew. But it made their job more fun and kept them from killing particularly obnoxious clients and their guests.

Tally had tried to figure out who the Aunt Mary and Uncle Charlie would be at her wedding to Mitch and decided they must be relatives of his, because nobody in her life would have the gall to behave like that.

Chapter 27

While Tally was juggling spring weddings on Jekyll, Anna Maria was fuming in Vieques. Nothing had gone right in her life since Eduardo was killed – that's how she thought of it - Tally "killed" her brother by bringing her fiancé to the island.

On the night Eduardo died, he'd been rushing across the island to see that gringa bitch, according to Anna Maria when she ranted to her friends about it. Only she knew the truth, that she'd lied to her brother and told him Tally was still at Lazy Jack's when she wasn't.

Some little rational part of her brain realized she had culpability for Eduardo jumping in his Jeep, drunk, to barrel across the island. But she erased the last text messages they'd exchanged from her phone – his was destroyed in the fiery crash – and that factoid would remain her secret. Soon, she forgot that it had ever happened. She publicly blamed the gringa wedding planner for Eduardo's death and told anybody who would listen that if she ever saw Tally again, she'd kill her on the spot.

"*Puta* needs some Viequenses justice," she'd raged.

Yaya got that gossip from her sister on their daily catchup call in early May, but she didn't share it with Tally. She decided her friend had enough on her plate with May brides and her own wedding now just weeks away. As long as Anna Maria was making those threats in Puerto Rico, Tally didn't need to know about it. She contemplated telling Mitch separately, but figured he'd spill the beans to his bride... so she didn't.

Tally was busy making weddings happen and dreaming about the honeymoon she and Mitch were planning to take eventually. They'd decided together that going away right after their wedding was a bad idea. Tally wanted time off on the front-end, and Mitch only had so much annual leave to cash in. Instead, they were going to check into a suite at The Cloister for the weekend. Cheryl had hooked them up with an amazing discount since she worked there.

Cheryl and Yaya were hosting Tally's bridal shower in one of the wine cellars at The Cloister. Tally had been overwhelmed and concerned about the cost before she found out exactly how much of a discount her childhood bestie had. It was going to be elegant – about two dozen women in total had been invited – and they were some of the most important people in Tally and Mitch's lives. Not all of her girlfriends were coming to town for it, but she knew several had mailed gifts down to Yaya to bring to the shower. She would see all of them in person at her wedding in a few weeks.

Her wedding gown was living on a hanger in Etah's condo, away from Mitch's prying eyes. Cheryl and Yaya had gotten their bridesmaid dresses already, and Cristie and Abby would go for their final fittings on Sunday, the day after the bridal shower. Tally had almost gone with pale yellow for her bridesmaids – it just worked for a May wedding, she thought – but Abby had put her foot down.

"I know it's *your* wedding but I look like death in yellow. Please pick any other color," she begged when Tally texted her a link to the first dress she'd chosen.

Out of respect for Abby – who had let Tally choose her own maid of honor dress for her wedding to Todd a few years earlier – she switched the yellow to a pretty shade of blue, and gave the girls a couple of styles to choose from. Everybody sent their measurements to the bridal shop in Savannah before the deadline, and the dresses arrived in plenty of time for any necessary fixes. The cornflower blue fabric was pretty on all of the women and a subtle nod to the police family she was joining. She was still considering putting a blue ribbon around the cake, as she had joked. Now, it would match the girls' dresses.

Tally's dress, when she finally found it, was gorgeous. It was an ivory silk satin – Etah had browbeat her into wearing silk. The gown was an A-line with a big train. It was absolutely plain except for a band around the sleeveless neckline that held tiny, hand-sewn crystals in the shape of sand dollars and starfish. There were crystals sewn onto her train as well. She loved everything about it. She'd seen the dress in a shop in Atlanta and tried it on. But it had a pleated band around the top that didn't suit Tally's style, even though the actual dress looked really good on her. She'd seen a pretty band of sea-themed crystals on a flower girl dress in the shop and ask her saleswoman about it. It turned out it was made by the same designer, and for a slightly unreasonable fee, they would switch the band at the top of the wedding gown to the beach-themed crystals instead of the pleat. Tally loved it even more than she'd imagined when she tried it on at her fitting. It was perfect.

She'd found a gorgeous coral Yves Saint Laurent suit with seashells in the embroidered fabric for Aunt Etah in another shop in Savannah and bought it on the spot. Fortunately, it fit Etah and all she'd needed to get was shoes and a bag to match.

"I knew it was perfect the moment I saw it. I'm so glad you like it," Tally told her aunt as she hung the outfit back up after Etah tried it on.

"I have to admit I was skeptical about a dress suit with shells on it but you were right, this is gorgeous," she looked closely at the fabric. "I'm actually going to be able to wear this again," she joked knowing Tally would find it hilarious.

"No bridesmaid ever actually wore a dress again that the bride thought they would get so much use out of," Tally had preached many times. She always told her brides to choose the least expensive dress they really liked because it was a one-and-done.

Tally and Mitch were getting married on the riverfront lawn of the historic Jekyll Island Club Hotel, just before sunset on May 30th. There would be cocktails on the lawn while the wedding party was taking pictures. Then they were having a formal reception in the Grand Dining Room. No receiving line. Tally thought they were a huge waste of time. She'd heard many brides say they'd wished they'd skipped the tradition, but she'd never heard a client say, "I wish I'd had a receiving line" afterwards. Some traditions were better dead, in her opinion.

In order to fit their group in the Grand Dining Room, they'd had to switch out all the historic furniture for tables and chairs that would hold everybody. The furniture, some of it original and some of it reproductions, took up a ton of unnecessary floor space. Removing the furniture was totally against hotel policy. In fact, it was in the written rules the hotel gave potential clients. But the furniture swap idea had come from the general manager, Mayra, who wanted her friend to be able to hold her wedding in one of the club's prettiest venues.

Fortunately, the rental company Tally had used for several years for her clients only charged her their costs to deliver and pick up the tables and chairs she needed, so that made switching the furniture affordable.

Mayra promised to have hotel staff move the furniture after breakfast was over for the hotel guests that morning. It would have been easier to have their wedding reception in the Morgan Center because it would easily hold far more than their number of guests and could be set up well ahead. But Tally felt like it wasn't the right vibe for their reception. It was a cool spot to be sure, but she'd spent too much time twiddling her thumbs during receptions in that venue while she looked at the exposed ceiling beams in what was originally an indoor tennis court. She couldn't imagine holding her own wedding reception there after working at so many others.

If a bride on a budget had wanted to do the things that Tally and Mitch were doing for their own wedding, she would have shut it down. No way would she have recommended all the required changes and upgrades she was making to a bride who was actually paying full price for it. But several of her vendors had really come through for Tally's big day, and she felt super lucky and appreciated.

Potomac Floral Wholesale, the biggest supplier to Jekyll Flowers, had given them an incredible deal on all of her wedding blooms. She basically only had to pay the shipping. A regular bride would have spent $5,000 to get what Tally was going to have for a few hundred.

Mayra worked the reception contract out in the most favorable way possible for Tally and Mitch. Add her club membership discount to that, and they were getting a deal that was basically unheard of. Mayra had also told Tally not to worry about the cost of her extras – like the furniture moving – she said the hotel would comp that stuff because they had such a close relationship. More than once, Tally had thanked her lucky stars that she was dealing with a friend at the hotel rather than the jerk who'd run off Cheryl.

They had agreed to just have her favorite DJ at their reception, and he was hardly charging anything as his gift to Tally. They'd decided to have a band on the deck at The Wharf after their rehearsal dinner instead of live music at the wedding. It was hard to time live music at a wedding with band breaks and toasts and special dances, so you really needed both if you didn't want dead time. Tally convinced Mitch they could have the best of both worlds by asking his buddy's band to play the night before their wedding and having a playlist of all their favorites queued up for the big day. There were quite a few of his trooper friends who couldn't come to the wedding but would be at the rehearsal dinner.

On their wedding day, most grooms played golf on one of Jekyll Island's historic courses while the ladies lunched and got ready for the main event. But not the Durham men, apparently. Mitch was following his older brothers' tradition of going shooting together before the wedding. Pete was handling the plans for all of that and Tally had tagged out. She told him she didn't care what they did, but he needed to have Mitch clean, properly dressed, and not sporting any new cuts or bruises by 4 p.m. on May 30th. That was when the wedding photographers would arrive to take their pictures.

Out-of-town guests were treated to trolley tours of the historic district and free passes to mini golf while they were on the island. They all got tickets to the Georgia Sea Turtle Center in their welcome bags, too. Nobody would be bored, but Tally wanted to make sure they had enough activities available so that she wouldn't have to figure anything out for anybody during her wedding weekend.

Considering she'd planned more than 100 weddings before her own, Tally was remarkably nervous about her nuptials. When she'd confessed as much to Mitch, he'd suggested that perhaps she knew too much about weddings and what could go wrong. He said "normal" brides didn't worry about the details they never knew about because Tally did it for them.

But she couldn't seem to let Kayla and Yaya step into her shoes for her wedding, even though she knew that's what she needed to do. She'd talked to her girlfriends about it, and Cristie had promised that she and Abby would keep her mind busy with other things when the day came. Tally had written and confirmed, and rewritten and reconfirmed, their wedding weekend schedule with every vendor. The only thing that could go wrong would be a sick or too drunk guest, and those weren't things she could control, no matter how diligent she was with her preparations.

Chapter 28

"No fucking way," Anna Maria raged to Nydia, who'd just shown her Yaya's social media posts about the bridal shower on Sea Island that Cheryl had thrown for Tally.

"It's a pretty place," Nydia said, scrolling. That just pissed her friend off even more.

"She doesn't deserve that. Or anything else she's getting. She should be six feet under the ground like my brother," Anna Maria declared, not for the first time.

Nydia just let her friend rant until she got distracted by something else. This was how it worked now – Anna Maria would curse Tally at least once a day, more if they'd been day-drinking. Eduardo's mother hadn't recovered from losing her precious son, and she rarely came outside of their house. His father sat on the front steps all day and made no effort to camouflage the liquor bottles that he drank from. He'd stopped bothering to put it in a glass after his only son was gone.

If they weren't both dating drug dealers in the same gang on the island, she would probably take a break from her childhood friend, because Anna Maria had started to sound like a broken record. She reminded Nydia a little bit of the crazy guy who fought with nobody – full-on boxing matches – on the corner by El Encanto. The maddest she'd seen Anna Maria get was when she'd suggested it was time for her to move on. Nydia had avoided her for a couple of days in the hope that she'd calm down but it wasn't an option right now because they were working together, keeping an eye out for anybody who shouldn't be rolling up their road in Luquillo.

Neither one of the girls had been dating their current boyfriend for very long, but they'd exclusively dated men that were affiliated with this particular drug family since high school. There was another drug organization on the island, and they were constantly at war with each other. But that's what the government got for failing to put patrol boats anywhere around Vieques. The local police didn't even have a boat – they had to call for one from the big island or borrow one from the federal Fish & Wildlife cops if they needed it for a rescue or investigation.

She heard Anna Maria muttering to herself in Spanish again and tuned back in when she heard her mention their boyfriends' names.

"No, Anna Maria, you don't want to do that," Nydia told her in a serious voice. "You even mention that like a joke and some night when they've done too much coke, they're going to do something about it for you."

"Maybe that's what I want. Then when Papi asks me if I had anything to do with it, I can look at him and honestly say no."

"That would be a lie though," Nydia pointed out. She lit a cigarette for Anna Maria and passed it to her, then she lit another for herself. They were sitting on her parents' front porch because it had a really good view of their corner.

"If you start this, you're in it. And Davio is fucking nuts. You know that. If you tell him you want him to kill somebody for you, he will," she warned.

"She isn't even in Puerto Rico," Anna Maria said dismissively.

"That hasn't stopped him in the past, and you know it," Nydia tried to douse her friend with a bucket of good cold, wet truth but she wasn't having it. Her pain at losing Eduardo had morphed into an unhealthy grudge.

"She's getting married really soon."

"I know."

"Eduardo will never get married or have a chance to be a father," Anna Maria said.

"That's not all Tally's fault," Nydia started to remind her friend but stopped when Anna Maria glared at her.

"How can you say that?" she raged. "If Tally hadn't left him, Eduardo wouldn't have turned to alcohol to numb his pain." She sounded so self-righteous that Nydia had to look away to hide a laugh. Eduardo had been a mess in high school and, if they were being honest, the most balanced time in his life had been the time he spent living with Tally, because she didn't like to hang out with his old crew. But Nydia didn't think it would be a good idea to point that out to his sister.

Anna Maria was on a roll. "She broke his heart. She left at the worst possible time. And then when her life turned out great, she brought back her new lover to rub it in Eduardo's face."

"Well, I'd still be careful about how worked up you get Davio over this. If he thinks he's not getting any because you're all sad about Eduardo, he might do whatever he can to make you happy," Nydia warned.

"Isn't that what a good boyfriend is supposed to do?"

"Not when it means killing somebody you don't like. That's like crazy-people extreme."

Anna Maria shrugged and looked at her as if to say "go ahead and call me crazy to my face" so Nydia let it drop. She certainly didn't want to bicker with her old friend over something that wasn't really her business.

"Besides, I'd want to do it myself. Why would I let Davio have all the fun?"

Nydia let the conversation go because there was nothing she could say in response to that. Before Anna Maria could bring it up again, her mother interrupted them to tell her to hang up the laundry.

While she did that, Anna Maria took a stroll up the hill to have a little chat with Davio.

Chapter 29

Tally and Kayla were prepping for the last big wedding they had to execute before they'd blocked off time ahead of Mitch and Tally's wedding. The clients – Jennifer Shuster and Bruce Whitney- were absolutely hilarious and the girls loved every minute of working with them.

Jen and Bruce chose Jekyll Island for their big day because it was where they first met, while hunting for treasure.

For many years, local fisherman used glass floats to help them identify their fishing nets in the water. It wasn't uncommon for the balls to break loose and wash ashore on Jekyll. Beachcombers who found the glass balls considered them a real treasure, and the Jekyll Island Authority had capitalized on that and instituted an annual treasure hunt on the island to find treasure balls.

The treasure hunt ran through all of January and February every year. It was heavily promoted and drew tourists from all over. Lots of Georgians remember the magical experience of an annual pilgrimage to Jekyll to look for "treasure" with their parents. It was a brilliant way to draw visitors – and increase their gate revenue - to the state park when it wasn't really beach weather.

The way it worked, volunteers hid clear plastic balls in random spots around the island early each morning for two months, and the lucky people who found them went to the visitor center to trade them for beautiful, hand-blown glass globes. The gift shop there also sold the pretty treasure balls for crazy prices to desperate folks who were willing to buy their own.

Bruce told Tally he was hunting for treasure balls near Glory Beach on a cold, windy morning when he bumped into Jen, who was also searching for treasure on Jekyll. They started chatting, and he invited her to go get coffee with him and warm up after they were done looking for "treasure."

"She said 'yes' and I was like 'sweet, she's hot and she doesn't think I'm weird to be out here hunting for plastic balls," Bruce laughed as he told the story. "And just then, we both spotted the same plastic ball under the steps up to the beach."

"I saw it first," Jen insisted. "He only spotted it because he looked to see what I was staring at."

"Doesn't matter. I let her keep it," Bruce continued. "We went to turn in the plastic ball together. She said I could take a picture with it, too, to prove I'd found it with her, even though she was taking it home. She ended up taking me home with her, too. And I never left."

They'd told their wedding planners the whole story at the first consultation and Tally had come up with a wedding plan that incorporated their history, and that of the island. There was only one complication – they really wanted to get married on the beach when the weather was warm. Which meant they couldn't get married during the months the treasure hunt actually happened.

Undaunted, Tally and Kayla had a great time creating a Treasure Wedding weekend for Jen and Bruce in early May. Tally had briefly considered doing something similar for her own guests before deciding she wanted to stay away from themes altogether, except to the extent that she could work in the Thin Blue Line. When she'd bounced the idea off Mitch, he'd made some cheesy joke about her being his treasure, and Tally took it to mean the idea of guests doing a treasure hunt did not excite him.

Jen and Bruce's welcome party was a sunset booze cruise, and guests were encouraged to come in costume as pirates and wenches. Tally and Kayla would dress up, too, and as guests arrived, give them a treasure map and schedule for their weekend that would be explained to them during the party.

Tally had tracked down plastic balls that looked like the ones the authority used. Kayla had used her TV time for the past week to put messages inside them that read "Jen and Bruce are getting married! If you're not a wedding guest, please leave this ball where it is so you don't ruin our game. Thank you!" She'd contracted with a few of the artisans who made the globes for the real treasure hunt and ordered a bunch of small ones that incorporated the couple's wedding colors.

Guests were encouraged to start hunting for the plastic balls immediately, anywhere on the island and especially at wedding events. The bride's father found the first one on the pier after the boat docked at the end of the party. The treasure hunt went all weekend until the bride and groom said "I do" in a beautiful beach ceremony. The guests who brought plastic balls to the wedding would be rewarded with treasure at the reception.

Tally and Kayla had talked about marketing "Treasure Weddings" with pictures from the upcoming weekend. "If it goes well," Tally reminded her protégé.

"Why wouldn't it go well?"

"Stop. You're going to jinx us," Tally was entirely serious. "Don't do it. We won't know if all of this was a good idea until after the wedding is finished. What if nobody finds a ball?"

"That won't happen – we put notes in them," Kayla argued.

Tally rolled her eyes.

"Well, not everybody who finds one will be an asshole and keep it, so some of them will be found, at least." Kayla looked really worried and Tally felt bad. The notes inside the globes had been Kayla's idea, and it was a good one. Otherwise, beachcombers were likely to think the balls were leftovers from the winter hunt.

"I'm sure most of them will be found if we hide them right. Do not assume these are normal 'treasure hunters' like the crew that descends on Jekyll in January. These people are fun, but I don't see any of them hiking to Sharktooth Beach or the waterpark to look for a ball. So don't waste your time hiding them that well. Better to make it too easy than too hard," Tally advised.

"I should have hidden more at the welcome party," Kayla wailed.

"Stop second-guessing yourself. One was perfect," Tally assured her. "But you'll want to hide a few at each of their events going forward. It makes it easy that everybody is staying at the historic hotel because we can hide a few on the porches and in the bushes there. Maybe one under the big tree in the middle of the lawn, too?"

"I've made up a list of places. I don't think it will take too much time. Too bad the bride and groom wanted in on the game – I thought we were going to get off the hook when Bruce wanted to hide the treasure balls himself," Kayla chuckled.

"Yeah, me too. But Jen's a bright girl. She doesn't want to waste half her wedding weekend dealing with a game. I don't blame her. This is literally why she hired us."

Kayla looked a little ragged, Tally realized. They'd been going flat out for weeks to keep spring brides happy, and it was wearing on her wing-woman. Tally hadn't been sleeping much at all and was likely running on pure bridal adrenaline. She decided to show some mercy.

"Let me see your list of places to hide them," she put her hand out and Kayla passed her the note pad.

She pulled a pen out of her purse and checked off about six lines. Then she took a picture of the list with her phone before handing it back to Kayla.

"I'll take the ones that I marked and do them tonight. You take care of the rest," she said.

"Oh, Tally. You don't have to do that. You took the biggest ones off the list."

"I'll make Mitch help me. He's home tonight," Tally said. "If he doesn't want to, I'll threaten to have a treasure hunt at our wedding."

"Okay, but if you don't feel like doing some of them, give me the list back in the morning and I'll finish it."

"That won't happen," Tally promised. She counted out the plastic balls she'd need for the hiding spots on her list and put them into a bag, then she put the bag in her Jeep. She and Mitch could make fast work of the project and maybe get in a beach walk, too.

"I'm thinking this is going to be a really fun weekend," she told Kayla in a positive tone meants to boost the younger planner's spirits. Her friend was starting to look droopy.

The women said goodnight and climbed into their respective vehicles. Kayla headed her apartment on St. Simons Island, and Tally went home.

Chapter 30

Mitch was sitting on the couch watching "Law & Order," of course, when Tally got home. She explained their mission, and he enthusiastically agreed to be her partner-in-crime.

"If we do it fast, we should be back here in an hour," Tally said as she refilled her water bottle.

"We could take a cooler of beer with us and make it last a lot longer," Mitch joked.

"It's a school night," she replied in a serious tone. "Can't be partying while we have clients on the island." Mitch groaned in response.

He drove and Tally told him where to go, one stop at a time. When she asked him to stop at the gas station so she could hide some balls by the Dairy Queen there, he pulled into the back corner of the Circle K and tried to pretend he didn't know her while she found a good spot.

Mitch parked the truck when they got to the miniature golf course and got out to help her. They knew that a big group of guests with kids were playing first thing in the morning, so it was a great location for several treasures. They were both laughing when they got back in his truck, but Mitch wasn't amused when he heard their next destination.

"Horton Pond, Tally? At night?" Horton Pond had a bunch of alligators and there was a cool viewing platform that almost guaranteed visitors would get to see one during their trip to Jekyll. She wasn't too thrilled about going there at night, either, but she and Kayla needed to be on the other end of the island the next day, so better to have it done.

"Nobody's ever been eaten by an alligator on Jekyll," Tally said encouragingly as Mitch begrudging turned in the direction of Horton Pond. They both laughed because they'd been telling each other that since they were kids. It wasn't the first time either of them had gone there at night, but it wasn't something they voluntarily did as adults. Teenage boys took their dates there so the girls would cling to them in fear as they shined a flashlight around looking for creepy gator eyes. It was cheaper than going to a scary movie.

"Okay, I'll go hide it," Mitch said in a determined voice after they parked as close as they could to the path to the viewing platform.

"I'll do it," Tally stopped him.

"Nope. I promised Etah that I'd always keep you safe."

"Yeah, but I'll die if you get eaten so it sorta defeats the purpose," she jumped down from the truck. "You stay here so there's somebody to call 911 if I don't come back," she ordered and then shut the door. She turned on her flashlight and marched toward the viewing platform. She'd though about trying to put the treasure ball someplace along the path or at the base of the platform, but given that she was in the dark, and she didn't want any of the guests to get hurt trying to retrieve a plastic ball, she had to be satisfied with just putting one on the viewing platform. Whoever got there first couldn't miss it.

She didn't exactly run back to the truck, but she walked a lot faster than usual. Mitch was chuckling when she got back in.

"Did you see Mama Gator or Sargon?" he asked, referencing two of the more famous alligators at Horton.

"I didn't look for Mama Gator or any other gators. I leave them alone and they leave me alone. We have an agreement."

"Sure you do. Where are we headed next?" he asked as he stopped at the entrance to Beachview Drive.

"Driftwood Beach and then Clam Creek Pier after that," she said, looking at the list on her phone.

"Ooooo, Driftwood. Another creepy one in the dark. But at least nothing will try to eat us," Mitch joked.

"Always a plus," Tally agreed.

"Let's do the pier first and then we can take a walk on Driftwood after we complete our mission," he suggested. He smiled at her a little wickedly and she knew exactly what he had in mind. She'd been to Driftwood at night with a few boyfriends in her wild youth.

Chapter 31

Yaya worked late that night, too, at the flower shop getting ready for all of the weddings that weren't Jen and Bruce's. She was a victim of her own success, much to Tally's amusement. They hadn't ended up needing to rent the space next door for a boutique because her friend figured out a way to use every available inch of wall space in the flower shop. To be honest, Tally felt a little claustrophobic on that side of the counter now, but tourists treated it like one more stop on their vacation list and came in to buy all sorts of things. Yaya found herself working late a lot of the time because she couldn't get flowers done and manage the cash register at the same time. They were going to need to hire a salesperson to man the counter soon.

The shop sold an amazing array of beach towels because Tally had started ordering extras every time couples used them as welcome gifts at their weddings. They had everything from Lilly Pulitzer to a chalk body outline on pavement. Yaya had planned to stock whichever ones sold fastest, but it turned out that every towel she put on display was gone within two weeks. The same thing happened with the tote bags. When couples had their wedding dates embroidered on them, she'd ordered some that just read "Jekyll Island" and they sold out faster than the beach towels.

Yaya had a few more things to do before she could call it a night. Since most of it was flower work, she called her cousin Lucia to gossip while she worked. Lucia still lived on Vieques, so her gossip was even better than the tea she got when she talked to mother and sister.

"Did you hear that Guillermo got shot the other night? He's dead," Lucia reported.

"I saw the news about it on Facebook but I haven't talked to anybody. I figured it was the usual drug war crap."

"I don't know, Yaya," Lucia said. "This was different. And nobody has seen Davio or Anna Maria since."

The last part of that caught Yaya's attention. "What? Why? How are they involved?"

"Guillermo was standing in front of his baby mama's house in Monte Santo, holding a kid, and somebody started shooting at him. Got him with the first shot, I heard, but the guy kept shooting."

"What about the baby?"

"It was a toddler and Guillermo dropped him after the first bullet went through his head. That was probably good though because the other bullets got him in the chest so it probably would have hit the baby," Lucia explained as calmly as if she was reporting the weather.

"*Ay Dios mio*," Yaya said.

"Yeah. I know his girlfriend and she's pretty shook up. She won't go back to the house. His father won't let anybody wash the blood and brains off the side of it, either. He's not cooperating with *la policia* and has vowed retribution through Viequenses justice."

"Great. Just what the island needs. A little more vigilantism," she shook her head to herself.

"That how we do."

"So do they think Davio shot Guillermo? How does he figure in here?" Yaya asked. "I thought they were friends."

"That was a long time ago, *amiga.* Guillermo's family has worked for the crew in Villa Hugo for years," she referenced the neighborhood located next to the new cemetery on Vieques. "Davio has always lived in Luquillo, so you know what that means. Friends become competitors and maybe even enemies. *No se que paso,"* she added.

Getting details out of Lucia was like pulling teeth, Yaya thought, as her cousin went into detail about what the dead man's baby mama was going to wear to the funeral the next day.

"And they think Davio shot him?" Yaya asked again.

"Yeah, they think it was Davio, or he got one of his boys from St. Croix to do it. Davio is a sharpshooter, or so he has always claimed. I dunno. There were shots, and then the sound of a motorcycle, and then nothing.

"Cops think the bad guy had a boat waiting," Lucia continued. "Guillermo's boys think Davio was in that boat. Nobody has seen Anna Maria since that night, either. Not that that's a bad thing – she's such a *puta* – but it's *muy interesante* that they've both gone missing *en el mismo tiempo.*"

Listening to Lucia made Yaya a little homesick. Puerto Ricans spoke Spanglish most of the time, even to each other.

"Yeah, that's shady," Yaya said. "But I heard she's been whack since Edwardo ran himself into a pole."

"Well, she was whack before that," Lucia said, making Yaya laugh. "But she's definitely been worse. Most of the old crew just tries to avoid her as much as we can. She started dating Davio after Eduardo died, and there's rumors that she's pregnant with his baby now. Dunno if that's true, so don't tell nobody that."

"No problem." Yaya figured she was probably the tenth person to hear that news so far that day. *Bochinche* – the Spanish word for gossip – was local currency on Vieques. There wasn't a whole lot to do after work except drink and swap stories.

When she got off the phone with Lucia, Yaya looked at her watch and thought about who she could call to find out more about what Anna Maria might be up to. She wanted to get the info without drawing any attention and decided she'd call her friend in St. Croix in the morning and see if Davio and Anna Maria had been seen by anybody she knew on the island across the water from Vieques. They'd either have left St. Croix or holed up with a friend. If the hit on Guillermo had come from high up in the Luquillo organization, it was possible they'd gone somewhere else. She'd check in with a few of her girlfriends in Vieques in the morning when she could build her questions into other conversations. It would seem weird if she called out of the blue asking about Anna Maria, given her connection to Eduardo's ex.

She thought about texting Tally to share the gossip but didn't, on the off chance her boss and bestie was already asleep with that hot man of hers. She knew her ringer would be turned on in case the Treasure Wedding guests needed her. She wasn't even sure if Tally knew who Guillermo was, not that it mattered. At this point, it was really just gossip and nothing that needed to be reported until the next day.

When she went to bed that night, Yaya couldn't shake the icky feeling she'd had her stomach since hearing the news from Lucia. She had a pretty good gut instinct usually. This time, she had no idea what it was telling her.

Chapter 32

The Treasure Wedding theme was a complete success, Tally decided, as she sipped coffee on the porch outside The Pantry at the Jekyll Island Club Hotel. She wasn't going to say it out loud and jinx it, but she was pretty sure their clients were blissfully happy. In fact, Jen and Bruce's friends were having so much fun that she secretly wished she'd incorporated the beautiful glass globes into her own wedding, despite Mitch's objections.

She went over to the wedding venue the next morning to review some last-minute notes with Mayra and spotted two wedding guests triumphantly carrying their plastic balls around the hotel with them like trophies. Their grins were infectious and Tally found herself lollygagging, counting the days until her own wedding in this beautiful historic spot.

Tally leaned over the railing for a better look, and she was pretty sure she spotted the mother of the groom in the bushes in the courtyard, perhaps looking for treasure... or lost keys. She giggled because whoever it was had already showed her arse to the world, so Tally decided not to call out to say hello and draw more attention to her.

"I'm sorry, I'm sorry," Mayra said as she rushed across the porch and greeted Tally with a kiss on the cheek. "I didn't mean to make you wait.

I was dealing with a little HR issue that I wanted resolved last week. Why does everybody make me be the mean guy?"

"Because you're so good at it," Tally smiled. "How's everything going with the Shuster/Whitney wedding? I love the couple and their guests seem pretty easygoing so far." The women worked closely to set up big contracts for lot of events on the property and Mayra knew exactly what Tally meant.

"Oh, they're great," she agreed. "I heard they were really funny last night after the pirate cruise. Everybody hunting for the balls in their costumes."

"Oh no," Tally burst out laughing. "We didn't actually start putting the balls out til late last night because we weren't expecting that much enthusiasm. Oops. Guess we'll have to see if they find the ones Kayla planted this morning. I could see one from the portico when I left my car with the valet."

"This really is a fun one," Mayra said. "I hope you do it again."

They reviewed the wedding day schedule together one last time. It wasn't complicated. The ceremony would be held on Glory Beach because that was where the bride and groom met – the hotel wasn't involved with any of that, except for the shuttles the couple had arranged to carry the guests to and from the walkway up to the beach.

The hotel would take care of everything related to cocktails and dinner in the garden and on the lawn, respectively, at Crane Cottage. They'd wrap it up with a farewell brunch in the Grand Dining Room on Sunday. Tally was going to keep the trains running on time through the Shuster/Whitney event without Kayla because the other planner was juggling two elopements on Driftwood Beach that they'd jammed into the schedule at the last minute.

The only trick to the Shuster/Whitney beach ceremony was getting the bridal party there without anybody seeing Jen's dress. Ideally, if everybody

was on time, the girls would be waiting in their vehicle on the other side
of the parking lot, watching guests arrive until it was time to get Jen out
and fluff up her dress. It would go great if everybody was where they were
supposed to be when they were supposed to be there. She had a hunch
that Bruce might even be early. She'd never seen a groom so excited to get
married.

It was a long wedding day for Tally because she'd had a lot of details she
needed to make sure weren't forgotten in the chaos of setup and everybody's excitement. More than once in the past, a best man had forgotten
to actually put the wedding rings in his pocket, so that sort of thing was on
her checklist, too, in addition to the decor. If she reminded them enough
times during the wedding weekend, the best man would not forget the
rings because they feared the wedding planner's wrath.

She anticipated zero problems with Jen and Bruce's friends. So far,
although there had been an open bar at everything, nobody had gotten
obnoxiously drunk. They had not yet identified Uncle Charley, although
Aunt Mary had been bugging the crap out of the hotel staff all weekend.
Tally had encountered her three times in the hour she was there to meet
with Mayra. She was on high alert to avoid her, now. She'd pointed the
guest out to Kayla at the rehearsal dinner and the younger planner agreed
the woman was definitely a contender for the title.

The beach ceremony setup was pretty simple. Just chairs for the guests.
No flower arch or tables or aisle runner that would try to trip the bride
on the sand. The bride's brother played the guitar, so he was going to play
"Brown Eyed Girl" as his sister walked down the aisle on his father's arm,
and then play David Bowie's "Changes" when the bride and groom recessed
after the ceremony. Tally had dropped off the men's boutonnieres at the
hotel room where they were getting ready earlier in the day so she wouldn't
forget, and she had the bride and bridesmaids' bouquets with her to give

them when they arrived at Glory Beach. Everything on her checklist was ready to go.

Tally had expected it to be a windy day so she'd worn pants and pulled her long curly hair into a tight French braid. It wasn't the most attractive look on her – Mitch had raised an eyebrow when he saw her leaving the house – but it was fully functional. She couldn't risk wearing a dress that might blow over her head while she was carrying something with both hands that she couldn't drop – like a tray with the sand blending ceremony on it, or something like that. She had too much hair to wear it down – by the time the guests arrived, she'd look like she'd been through a wind tunnel. So, she was going chic and tight and making sure everything on her was tied down in case she had to grab something that wasn't.

"I should have brought a book," she texted Kayla from the parking lot at Glory Beach. Kayla didn't reply because she was trying to orchestrate an elopement at the other end of Jekyll Island at the same time. Tally gave herself a mental slap on the wrist for being annoying when her employee needed to concentrate.

A couple of minutes later, the groomsmen arrived in the parking lot, honking as they pulled in. It was a rowdy, goofy bunch of guys but they quickly got their acts together when guests began arriving. The gentlemen took turns escorting the ladies up the boardwalk to the beach and then returned to pick up another guest to seat. It was a relatively long walk, and the men made multiple jokes about how they were getting their steps in at this wedding.

The bride's parents were the last to arrive, as had been planned on the schedule that clients rarely followed. The Shuster/Whitney wedding was a rare exception and Tally loved it. As soon as Bruce returned from seating his own parents, he took his soon-to-be mother-in-law's arm and headed back, with the photographer snapping away in front of them. Tally looked at her watch and remembered why they rarely did weddings at Glory Beach. It was a long walk and just getting the wedding started took forever.

Jen's dad waited patiently in the parking lot for his baby girl to arrive so he could walk her down the aisle. Mr. Shuster looked handsome in a blue seersucker suit. The groom didn't want to wear a tie on his wedding day, so nobody else did, either.

"I'm loving this," the father of the bride told Tally at the rehearsal dinner, as he stood on the deck wearing khaki shorts and a golf shirt. "This destination wedding thing works for me. When my son got married, I had to wear a penguin suit all day and I was miserable – but gotta do what the future daughter-in-law wants, right?"

"Absolutely," Tally agreed.

"My daughter isn't as uptight as my daughter-in-law," he said in a confidential tone. "She's been a lot more fun with all this wedding stuff."

Just then, a big black SUV pulled into the parking lot. Tally assumed it was the bridal party until it passed them and kept going to the other end of the vast parking lot. Jen and her girlfriends were in another overflowing SUV right behind it and Tally focused on the project at hand – getting Jen and her dress out of the vehicle without hurting either of them.

The bride looked amazing. Jen had the same kind of long, blond curly hair as Tally, and her wedding planner had been skeptical when she'd heard the bride planned to wear it down on the beach. But Jen used a headband to hold her veil that also held her hair back and out of her face. Tally's own veil was a family heirloom on loan from Bonnie – Roberta and Robin had both worn it and she was honored to join the tradition – but the cathedral length veil attached with a comb. She wondered if she could somehow retrofit it for a simple headband like Jen was wearing.

To save time, the bride, the bridesmaids, the photographers, and the wedding planner trudged as far down the catwalk together as they could go without the wedding guests being able to see them. From that point, the bridesmaids walked down the aisle one after the other. If Tally timed it right, Jen and her dad would appear at the top of the stairs to the beach at about the same time the last bridesmaid took her place up front.

She'd have preferred to have Kayla there to spot her from the ceremony and tell her when to say "go," and she made a mental note to make sure they always had two people – in addition to the minister and photogs – on hand to send a bride down the aisle at Glory Beach in the future. She'd said as much to Mitch and almost asked him to come along and help her, but he needed to take paperwork over to his office in Brunswick and he'd already helped hide the treasure balls. He never asked her to come to work with him and she didn't want to make a habit of asking him to be a wedding planner.

<h1 style="text-align:center">Chapter 33</h1>

Mitch was approaching the gate on the Jekyll causeway when he saw emergency lights headed toward him. They were coming from the Brunswick side of the causeway, not from the trooper barracks located in the same building as the Jekyll Island Visitor Center, right next to the gate. He looked over and saw there were no GSP vehicles parked outside Post 35, and that made the hairs on the back of his neck stand up. There were always patrol vehicles in that parking lot.

He pulled in and stopped his truck long enough to grab his radio out of his go-bag. His father would give him a lecture for needing to do that – Tom preached turning on your radio and scanner whenever you were in a car in your jurisdiction. He did it in his patrol car and his POV (that's cop talk for personally-owed vehicle) and strongly recommended that his sons do the same. And they all did, most of the time.

Mitch watched as several Georgia State Patrol cars, marked and unmarked, slowed down and stopped to wait for the gate to open for them. There were a few Glynn County Sheriff's Office cars behind the state troopers, and several unmarked cars behind them that he thought might be feds, based on the license plates. Mitch noticed that the police cars turned off their sirens as they approached the gate and didn't turn them back on after they passed through. He wondered what that was about. He switched between channels looking for any kind of chatter on the police radio.

Something hinky was up, and he wasn't hearing anything about it on the air. He called his dad as he pulled back onto the causeway in the direction from which he'd come. It was probably no big deal and he was being stupid, but he'd feel better about things if he checked on Tally. He also wanted to know what was going on with all the police cars. The cameras and the gate fee generally served as a crime deterrent.

Tom's phone went straight to voicemail so Mitch hung up and sent a text. He had just pulled into the soccer complex parking lot that led to Glory Beach when his phone pinged. Mitch parked his truck next to Tally's Jeep and made a point not to let his horn honk when he locked it. He figured the sound wouldn't carry that far, but he wasn't going to risk being the one to interrupt a wedding ceremony.

He picked up his phone to see who had messaged him before he got out of his vehicle. It was a response from his dad.

"Not sure what's happening. It was an ATF operation and nobody bothered to alert the locals because it didn't initially go down on Jekyll. That's the skinny here. But I can ask around and see what else I can find out. I'm at Betty's," Tom added to the end of the text, naming a cop hangout bar located close to the Federal Law Enforcement Training Center. Perfect, Mitch thought. Somebody from FLETC would have the answer.

Mitch didn't wait to hear back from his dad. His gut wouldn't let him. Instead, he headed up the long walkway to the beach at a jog. He came around a gentle bend on a rise in the path between trees and saw several things all at once that made him stop.

The bride was walking toward the staircase to the beach, on her father's arm. Tally stood about 20 yards back, where she couldn't be seen by the guests, and to her right – in the dunes where no one was supposed to be – was man dressed entirely in black. From where Tally was standing, the man was entirely camouflaged by tall grasses. But from where Mitch was standing, he could clearly see the suspect on his knees, pointing a rife in the direction of the woman he loved.

It didn't make sense, but Mitch didn't wait for things to compute before he started moving. He looked at the distance between himself and the armed man, and the woman he was supposed to be marrying in two weeks, and he went into action. He took one second to send his father a text telling him to send backup. and then he took off in the direction of the beach.

The wind Tally had worried would make her hair look horrible at the wedding worked to Mitch's advantage as he powered across the dunes toward the crouching man. He could hear strains of a guitar coming from the beach and knew it meant the breeze was coming inland from the water. The gunman was unlikely to hear Mitch behind him if he was careful. All those thoughts ran through his head as he sped through the soft sand and tall grass.

He could see the gunman hefting his weapon a bit higher as he sighted in his target, and Mitch forgot about not making noise. It occurred to him that he could gun-face the suspect and order him to drop his weapon, but the suspect had a higher-caliber weapon and might shoot Tally *and* Mitch. He made up his mind on the fly, and two giant steps later, he launched himself at the gunman from behind. As they fell, he grabbed the man's rifle and tried to take it from him.

The gunman fought back, refusing to let go of his weapon. The rifle got jammed down into the sand as they fought and then it fired. The suspect paused for a second and that gave Mitch a chance to smash the rifle into his head, knocking him off balance. Mitch grabbed the opportunity to pounce on the suspect's back and yanked his arms behind his back. He pulled two zip ties out of his back pocket, thinking "thank you Dad for telling me to always have handcuffs on my person because you never know when you might need them."

When the suspect he was sitting on stopped fighting, Mitch pulled out his phone and called his dad. He could hear sirens in the distance.

"Dad, situation is under control. I'm okay and I've got the suspect in custody. Can you ask them to turn off the sirens so they don't disrupt the wedding?"

Chapter 34

Tally heard the gunshot and whipped her head around to see what was going on behind her. It hadn't sounded like gunfire, really. More like a single firecracker. Then she spotted Mitch and the man he was sitting on, and the big rifle lying in the sand where Mitch had flung it away from them.

Mitch looked okay and he gestured for her to stay back. She glanced back over in the direction of the beach in time to see the bride's head disappear beyond the dune as her father helped her down the aisle. They hadn't heard anything. Good, she thought. She had no idea what was going on. She didn't know who Mitch was sitting on. She felt like she should run over and help him – she'd sworn she'd never be that wife who stands on the side while her spouse is getting his ass kicked – but he was telling her to stay back. She realized that in a few minutes, she might need to find a way to keep the guests on the beach after the ceremony.

She took the boardwalk toward Mitch but stopped when she saw a lot of law enforcement officers rushing up the path to him. He definitely didn't need her help, so she backtracked to her spot with a view of the ceremony and prayed the minister would take his time. She couldn't remember if it was a long ceremony. She couldn't remember the bride and groom's names at that very moment. What the holy hell was going on? Tally wanted to scream and freak out and do a million other histrionic things but she couldn't because for now, her clients were still blissfully unaware that there was some kind of police takedown happening in the dunes, ridiculously close to their wedding ceremony.

Tally saw the group of officers swarming around the suspect and Mitch. Mitch got up and then a couple of the men hauled the guy he'd been sitting on to his feet and began walking him toward the parking lot. When his backup had things under control, Mitch made his way over to the dune to Tally and kissed her.

"What was that about?" she was too stunned to process the fact that Mitch had thought that guy was going to shoot her. That hadn't even occurred to her yet. "Will they be gone before the guests are ready to leave in about...," she looked at her watch. "Another five minutes? It's windy and I don't expect anybody to hang out down there unless they're needed for family pictures."

Mitch looked at her like she was completely insane. But he recognized that she was in between and rock and a hard place. Whatever had just happened – and she was starting to suspect that Mitch didn't know what it was, either – could destroy the wedding for the bride and groom who probably had nothing to do with the incident taking place.

She gave him a pleading look and he broke.

"Fine," he said. "Lemme see what I can do."

She didn't see him again before the ceremony ended, and she assumed that meant he'd been able to clear out the parking lot. She was not entirely correct, although the guests didn't have the slightest clue about the real story.

There was a large group of law enforcement vehicles parked in the far corner of the lot, surrounding the black SUV that Tally had noticed right before the bridal party arrived.

"What's that about?" a guest asked.

"Police task force picnic," she replied, avoiding eye contact. She used that line with all of the guests who asked – gotta keep the stories straight, right? The bride and groom didn't even notice the police activity when they loaded up into their vehicle to go take pictures in front of the historic hotel. Tally called Mitch's cell phone the second after she closed the car door behind the couple.

"Are you here?" she asked, standing next to her Jeep and looking across the parking lot.

"I'm here," he replied at about the same time she saw his tall form exit the scrum of cops and head in her direction.

She met him halfway and threw her arms around him.

"Oh. My. God," she began, dramatically. "What just happened? Was he going to shoot my bride? Does she have a crazy ex we don't know about?" Everything that had been rushing through her head as she tried to hold it together for her clients came rushing out at Mitch.

He held her tightly for a moment and then released her and showed her his phone.

"Do you know either of these people?" Mitch asked, swiping.

Tally gasped. "No freaking way." All of the blood drained from her face.

"Is that a yes?" he tried to make light of the difficult moment with a smile, but quickly read the room and stopped. "Who are they, Tally?"

"They're both from Vieques," she said in a whisper. "I don't know his name but I've seen him on the island. And she's..." Tally paused.

"She's who?" Mitch asked.

"Eduardo's sister. Remember that girl who screamed at us in Lazy Jack's? That's her," she said with confidence.

"I thought I recognized her but I totally couldn't place her," Mitch said as the lightbulb went on for him, too.

"Why are they here?"

"We don't know anything yet, we're waiting on a translator," he explained.

Tally couldn't refrain from hooting in laughter. "They both speak perfect English."

"Of course they do," Mitch groaned.

Tally needed to head over to the hotel before the bride and groom finished pictures so that she could announce their grand entrance at the reception without anybody having missed her. She told Mitch and he understood.

"Look, call me when you're done for the night and I'll come get you, or you can meet me wherever I am. I have a feeling that this thing is bigger than we realize because there's a whole lot of federal agencies here that don't usually hang out on Jekyll Island. I'll find out what's going on and text you. But please, go straight to the hotel now. Park on the driveway at Crane Cottage – I know you don't usually do that but I feel like an extra ounce of caution is called for."

She kissed him and said goodbye, marveling at how much she loved Mitch as she drove away. He stood in the parking lot watching until she made the turn.

Tally called Yaya from the car and told her what happened and who was there. She was certain to know the culprits better than Tally – she should have said something to Mitch about that. Or Mitch already realized Yaya's connection which was why he hadn't asked about it. Either way, the girls talked until Tally turned left into the back entrance of the historic district.

"Will you just call Mitch now so he doesn't think I'm an idiot?" she asked.

"I'll call him as soon as we hang up. But that man will never think you're an idiot," Yaya laughed. "A trouble magnet, maybe. But not an idiot."

Chapter 35

Cocktails were in full swing when Tally arrived at Crane Cottage. Everybody looked happy and oblivious to the near disaster that had almost ruined Jen and Bruce's wedding. Tally was still shaken, although she was trying hard not to show it. She was more relieved than she wanted to admit when Kayla showed up before the bride and groom's entrance.

"What are you doing here? You're supposed to be off tonight," Tally used her teacher voice.

"Yaya called me."

"Oh," Tally understood. Her girls hadn't wanted her to be alone through the limbo of finishing up the wedding.

"She said to tell you she was going to meet Mitch at the police station and you should let me run things and meet them over there."

Tally didn't reply immediately, and when she did, she ignored what Kayla had said.

"Will you announce them?" she asked when she spotted the bride and groom making their way toward their reception.

"Sure," Kayla grabbed a copy of the event schedule to make sure she had the wording right. Couples were very particular about this one item and it could get dicey if the bride wasn't taking the groom's name. Of course, Jen and Bruce were easy.

Tally stopped the bride and groom before they got to the entrance, while Kayla cued the DJ. After making sure the photographers were in place, she gave the other planner a signal and Kayla turned on her microphone.

"Ladies and gentleman, please give a huge welcome to the new Mr. and Mrs. Bruce and Jennifer Whitney!" Kayla announced with a smile, gesturing to the far corner of the area. Then the DJ played the couple's entrance song and everybody applauded. The cocktail party resumed once Jen and Bruce said hello to their parents and friends.

"You don't have to hang around," Kayla reminded Tally a few minutes later when they were sitting on a wall watching their clients from a distance.

"I know I don't. But I really want to stay through the whole treasure ball giveaway thing. It's the first time doing it and I'd been wishing I'd have another set of hands here," she admitted.

"Well, I can't argue with that but I'm sure I could grab some of the hotel's service staff to help me if you want to leave," Kayla said.

"They're going to start seating for dinner in the big tent in a few minutes. Toasts are immediately afterward and then the treasure balls. Depending on how long people talk, I could be out of here in an hour."

"Ha!" Kayla didn't try to stifle her laugh. "There are so many toasts. I'll be glad I have my Kindle on my phone," she joked.

But Tally hadn't been far off on her guestimate. Alerted by Yaya, Mayra had swooped in to oversee the execution of things and the wedding reception went flawlessly. It wasn't much more than an hour later when they finished the toasts and were ready to move on to treasure balls. Everybody had been loving and appropriate in their speeches, which was nothing less than what Tally had expected from this couple's friends and family. She joked that the only thing missing from the Shuster/Whitney wedding was the obligatory obnoxiously drunk relative.

Kayla and Tally were excited about the treasure ball giveaway. There had been a lot of plastic balls hidden and the wedding planners thought most of them had been found. To avoid having plastic balls rolling around on the reception dinner tables, they'd asked guests to "check their balls" at the entrance. The signs were pretty hilarious. Anyone who'd found a treasure got their name put on the list when they dropped their ball into the bucket. Not terribly flashy but it did the job without making people jump through a bunch of dumb hoops.

The actual awarding of the treasure balls may have been the highlight of the wedding for everyone. Tally gave the bride the list of successful treasure hunters, and Jen held the microphone and announced the names while Bruce handed out the awards as if they were Golden Globes.

Each glass ball was packaged safely in its own box in the hope that the magical globes would make it to guests' homes in one piece. Tally and Kayla stood by on the side, passing boxes to the bride and groom, and then taking them back to hold while they hugged the recipients, then handing back the prizes again. The DJ played hysterical music throughout – everything from drum rolls to smashing glass that scared everybody.

It took longer than Tally had expected because the bride and groom had so much fun giving out the specially-ordered glass globes. Bruce and Jen posed for pictures with each guest, and several recipients took their fragile prizes out of the boxes to display in the photos, which made the process take even longer. But the bride and groom were ecstatic about it all and that made it totally worth the effort. Tally was relieved when the DJ finally turned the lights back down and called the wedding couple to the floor for their first dance.

She texted Mitch as she'd promised. "Do you want me to meet you somewhere?"

His reply was quick. "I'll pick you up."

"I'd rather not leave my car at Crane Cottage," she replied. It would look weird to the clients if her car was still there even though she was not.

"Okay, then I'll meet you at Crane and follow you home so you can drop off your car. No biggie."

Tally thanked Kayla again for covering for her, and then scooted out the back of the reception. She ran smack into the father of the bride, who was outside of the tent smoking a cigarette. Tally stopped to ask if he'd enjoyed himself and got a rave review. Mr. Shuster said he loved everything about his daughter's wedding and promised to send Jekyll Weddings all of his friends with daughters.

Tally had just gotten into her Jeep when she saw Mitch's truck in the driveway of Crane Cottage. He flashed his lights at her and she took that to mean, "go ahead." So, she went. And Mitch followed.

He pulled in directly behind her in their driveway but didn't get out of his truck.

"Do you want to go in and change first, or can we just leave now and I'll tell you what's going on on the way?" he asked through the window. The tone of the question suggested Tally's answer should be the latter.

"No, I'm fine," she said and walked to the passenger side of the big pickup to climb in. Mitch reached across the seat and gave her a hand.

Chapter 36

"Where are we going?" Tally asked after her door was shut and Mitch had put the truck in reverse. It was late, she was exhausted from the long day, and the turn of events had been disorienting.

"First stop is going to be the Post, because my dad is still over there and I promised him we'd come by and talk through things before we head over the causeway. Then we need to go to the FBI Field Office in Brunswick so you can give them a statement. The only way I could stop the agents from bothering you in the middle of the wedding was to promise we'd come over there and talk to them tonight. That's where they have the suspects in custody," he explained.

There was a lot to tell her and he wasn't sure how much of it he should dump on her while they were driving. When Tally didn't comment, he glanced over to make sure she was okay.

She was looking away from him out the window and he suspected that meant she was crying, but he didn't call her out on it. With everything that had happened in the last few hours, she had every right to cry. When she found out what had really happened out there at Glory Beach, she was going to be even more freaked out.

He stayed quiet for the rest of the short trip, except to ask her if she was hungry or thirsty. She wasn't. When they got to the state police barracks, he noticed she didn't jump right out of the truck. He walked around and opened the door for her, the way his mother had taught him he should do every time. He didn't wait for her to climb out, but instead put his hands on her waist, lifted her, and set her on her feet. She had a shell-shocked look on her face he'd never seen before and they'd been through a lot together.

"You ready to go in?" he asked. Tally's head snapped around so she faced him and she looked confused. "Are you ready to go inside and talk to them?" he asked again, but in a softer voice.

"Do I have a choice?" Tally asked.

Mitch stopped and looked at her. "Probably. If you're too wiped out to deal with this tonight, I can ask my dad to try and run interference for us." He wasn't dragging the woman he loved into an FBI interrogation when she looked like a rescued hostage. "But I think you are going to want to know what happened tonight sooner rather than later so you can process what you're feeling in context."

She shrugged but he took it for agreement, and they walked hand-in-hand into the station.

Tom Durham swept Tally up in a hug the moment he saw her. When he finally let go, he looked her in the eye and asked her how she was holding up.

"It's not my best day," she admitted. "I still don't know the whole story."

"You remember Andy, right?" her future father-in-law asked, gesturing to a familiar face sitting in a chair at the conference table.

"Of course, I do," Tally said, remembering her manners when she realized she wasn't just talking to her family. "It's half of my favorite detective duo, Johnson & Johnson." She smiled and extended her hand to the detective. He'd been part of the investigation team a year ago when her former client tried to burn down her flower shop.

Mitch wanted to step in and hold onto Tally, but he kept his mouth shut and watched as his dad guided her into a chair and placed a bottle of water in front of her. He noticed that the woman who told him she wasn't thirsty just five minutes earlier drank down the entire beverage in short order.

His dad hadn't asked if she wanted a drink because he was treating his future daughter-in-law like a crime victim and taking care of her instinctively, rather than forcing her to ask for help. Mitch felt stupid but all he could do was keep quiet and listen, and then be there for Tally when she needed him.

"Let's start with what you do know, Tally," Tom suggested, taking the seat next to her. "Okay if I sit here?" he asked after he sat down.

"Sure," Tally nodded as she said it, but her eyes still seemed a little bit vacant to Mitch. When nobody asked any questions, Tally started talking of her own volition.

"I have no idea what happened," she confessed. "I had just sent my bride down the aisle when I heard the crack of a gunshot behind me. It took me a few seconds to spot Mitch and the gunman on the dune, but they were fighting when I first saw them. Or at least that's how it looked, I was pretty far away at that point. Then a bunch of cops came running up and took the guy away, and I finished my wedding hoping nobody had heard anything. Speaking of which, why wasn't it louder?"

"The muzzle of the gun was buried in the sand when the weapon fired," Mitch explained.

"Oh," Tally thought about it before she continued. "The whole thing scared the crap out of me, but somehow I just kept thinking that there are no do-overs in weddings and odds are it had nothing to do with my clients. I owed it to the bride and groom to keep it together," she explained.

"Was that guy trying to shoot at me?" she asked the question that Mitch had been waiting for.

His dad answered it for him.

"Well, yes and no, Tally," Tom said. "Yes and no."

"Meaning?"

"Meaning Davio Rodriguez and Anna Maria Romero did come to Jekyll to kill you, but they had your wedding date wrong."

His words sunk in slowly. "Huh?"

"They thought today was your wedding and he was going to shoot the bride, not the wedding planner. I don't think he knew much about you, and you and that bride looked a lot alike from what Mitch told me," Tom continued. "It was actually pretty damned funny when his girlfriend figured out that the woman he'd gotten them arrested over wasn't you. She went bananas!"

"Oh my God, he would have killed Jen as she was walking down the aisle?" Tally stood up and headed for the bathroom, but she only made it as far as the trash can by the door of the conference room before she threw up. Mitch went to get her a paper towel while Tom and Andy looked away to give her a moment of privacy to pull it together.

She went into the ladies' room and washed her face, and then came back into the room a few minutes later.

"Okay, tell me everything. Let's get this over with. I've had enough of Eduardo's little sister for a lifetime. What the hell is Anna Maria doing in Georgia, on Jekyll Island of all places?" she sounded angry, which Mitch preferred over scared.

"They came here specifically to find you," Tom explained. "Davio is on the run because he's the prime suspect in a murder on Vieques. He's Anna Maria's boyfriend."

"Ah," Tally said. "So that's the connection. I don't even know that guy and I've been trying to puzzle out why he would try to kill me. Anna Maria hates my guts but I'm not sure I ever actually met her boyfriend."

Mitch finally joined the conversation. He knew more about the details of Tally's life than she did at that moment.

"I don't think that she's been dating him for that long. They weren't together when you and I were in Vieques, from what I picked up," he reported. "Yaya said he's a wanna-be big player in the Luquillo family."

"Where is Yaya?" Tally suddenly remembered her bff had told Kayla to tell Tally she was with Mitch.

"FBI, ATF, and police interviewed her here, and then I told her to go home and get some sleep. I suspect she was going to call everybody in Vieques and get to be the first one to tell everybody that Anna Maria got locked up."

"Oh, no doubt," Tally laughed. "Was she okay when she left?"

"She was fine. Just really angry that Anna Maria tried to kill you. She explained the whole 'Viequenses justice' thing to us but I'm pretty sure nobody but me understood what she was talking about. You really have to see Vieques and spend a little time there to 'get it,'" Mitch said.

"You really do," Tally agreed.

"Yaya knew more about the big picture on this than anybody," Mitch told Tally. "Without her help, we'd still be trying to figure out all the connections. But man, she knows everything and everyone. She called her dad to get some other numbers we needed for officials down there."

"Turns out that Davio killed somebody's baby daddy on Vieques, and Anna Maria must have done something, or made some big promises, to convince him to help her eliminate you. We're still figuring out how they got to Miami, but if Davio hadn't used his cell phone to buy that rifle, there's a good chance that your bride would be dead," Tom explained.

"He's a sharpshooter. Spent two years in the Army before he did something stupid that got him dishonorably discharged. Otherwise, he was going to be a sniper."

"Instead, he became a drug dealer," Tally said, shaking her head.

"Actually, Yaya seems to think he was always a drug dealer – says it was the family business - and the Army was just a hiatus from his chosen field," Mitch said.

"That makes more sense," Tally laughed. "She knows everything. Always has." The casual conversation about what had happened was weird, but she was starting to process what had happened and feel a little better.

"You lucked out, Tally," Tom told her. "If it weren't for several stupid mistakes they made along the way, I don't think Mitch would have been there to stop him."

"Wait a second. Why were you there?" Tally asked, suddenly realizing how backwards that was. There was zero reason for Mitch to have been at the wedding. But he'd been there exactly when she needed him.

"I was on my way into the office when I saw police cars racing onto Jekyll with their sirens off, and I had a weird feeling. So, I turned around to go check on you just to make sure everything was okay. And it wasn't."

"Well. thank God you had a feeling," Tally said, reaching over to squeeze his hand. He knew it was dawning on her that her fiancé had experienced the traumatic day right alongside her.

"Seriously."

"I'm so sorry about all of this..." she started to say, but literally everyone in the room shushed her.

"You don't owe anybody an apology, Tally," her future father-in-law interrupted. "I ain't gonna lie, you do attract some strange situations, but you don't do anything to bring it on yourself from what I've seen.

"Maybe after you and Mitch are married, he can figure out how to stop the weirdos from following you," Tom suggested.

"Or just shoot them," Andy chimed in. "Y'all don't live that far from Horton Pond."

That was a standing island joke. It was easy to get rid of a body on Jekyll if you knew where to take it. They all laughed but Tally hoped they'd never have to consider the option seriously since the pond allegedly had cameras.

"Look, it's after 11, and you guys still have to go over to Brunswick so Tally can give her statement to the alphabet agencies," Tom reminded them, referring to the FBI, ATF, and GBI. "You should probably get going and I'll call and let them know you're on the way."

"You're right," Mitch agreed, looking at his watch.

"Tally, they're not going to let Mitch participate in the investigation as a law enforcement officer because he's too close to it, and because it was his future wife they were trying to kill. However, he's a witness to everything and was the one who stopped the gunman so that means you can't have him in the room with you during interviews," Andy advised. "You're the victim here but sometimes feds forget that. Don't let them speak rudely to you or push you around. Your interview shouldn't be an interrogation and you can get up and walk out at any point."

Mitch could see concern clouding Tally's eyes, but she nodded in understanding to the detective.

"Do you have any questions before you go?" Andy asked her gently. Tally took a second to think about her answer and then looked at Mitch.

"Can we stop and get chocolate on the way?" she asked him.

"Absolutely."

Chapter 37

Mitch went to stay with his parents for the last few days before the wedding so that Tally's out-of-town besties could stay with her and do bride things that her fiancé would rather not know about. Tally knew there was a bachelor party planned and she wasn't concerned in the least. How much trouble could he get into with three groomsmen who were also law enforcement officers? She shook her head just thinking about it. The Durham boys could get into plenty of trouble if they tried, she answered herself and groaned.

It had been mad chaos for the past two weeks – first, they'd had to deal with the Anna Maria mess. But once they'd given everybody statements, there was nothing left to do. Puerto Rico wanted to extradite Davio back there to prosecute him for Guillermo's murder. However, the feds wanted to keep him stateside because the odds of a successful prosecution on gun charges and everything else in a federal court was much more likely than a conviction in the screwed-up justice system in Puerto Rico. The only advantage to sending Davio back to be prosecuted on the island was the knowledge that there was no air conditioning in the island's prisons. Only the federal lockups in Puerto Rico had AC. Either way, Davio was going to sweat for his crimes.

Tally spent a few days after the Shuster/Whitney wedding following up with vendors and communicating with clients to remind them that she would be away from her desk for the next three weeks. Urgent matters should be referred to Kayla, but she asked her clients to consider whether they had a real emergency because if they had to reach out, it would be Tally's wedding they were interrupting.

The week of Tally and Mitch's wedding was all about them – she wasn't even checking work emails. She'd posted a blog sharing what she was up to and announced she wouldn't be posting again until she could share her own wedding pictures with them in a couple of weeks.

On Monday, Tally and some of her girlfriends went to the spa at The Cloister as Cheryl's guests, and when they came out of there, she was waxed, buffed, polished, and ready for all of her upcoming wedding events.

Etah and Bonnie threw a bridal shower on Tuesday afternoon at her aunt's new condo. Her girlfriends had thrown a surprise lingerie shower for her a month earlier and the guests at Etah's luncheon were mostly Jekyll neighbors and Etah's old friends. It had been light and fun – tea sandwiches and champagne punch – and Etah and Mitch's grandmother's friends embarrassed her half to death with an aggressive game of "How Well Do You Know the Groom." Those women knew entirely too much – more than Tally wanted to know, if she were completely honest. She had a few questions for her soon-to-be-husband by the time the party was over.

Wednesday was her only quiet day and with a house full of girlfriends, there was nothing quiet about it. They managed to get in some pool time at the club, but Tally couldn't fully relax. She had a clipboard with all of her lists on it waiting at home, and she felt like she should be doing something – anything – to make sure her wedding to Mitch went flawlessly. But there wasn't more to do. It was all ready. Something would go wrong, she knew. Whether a vendor would run out of booze or a drunk guest would wreck a golf cart, she didn't know. But it would be something and with her luck, it wouldn't be something small. The tasks that she'd usually be doing for another bride at this point on the schedule weren't on Tally's to-do list. Yaya and Kayla were handling all of those little details and she wasn't even supposed to ask about their progress. They were professionals and would come to her if they ran into a problem, they'd reminded her each time she called to check on them.

On Thursday evening, Bonnie and Etah co-hosted a barbecue at Bonnie's house for family and all of the out-of-town guests who had arrived on Jekyll Island. Afterward, all of Mitch and Tally's friends went across the street to Etah's house – now Tally and Mitch's place – to drink and chat on the front porch late into the night. She'd finally thrown Mitch and his brothers out close to 2 a.m., after making sure they had a sober driver.

When Tally's alarm clock woke her on Friday morning, she turned it off quickly hoping that it hadn't woken up Cristie or Rita. Her girlfriends were both staying in guest rooms down the hall. Rita was trying out the murphy bed they'd just installed in Tally's old bedroom.

Tally wanted a chance to have her coffee on the deck by herself before she had to play hostess, not that either of her childhood friends expected anything from her. Tally wanted to re-check all of her wedding checklists in peace without anybody telling her to put them away. She knew Kayla had the vendors under control and that everything had been confirmed multiple times, but it was hard to just sit back and "be a bride," as everyone kept ordering her to do.

She took a long outside shower with the peekaboo window open and watched the pelicans. Tally spent far longer than was necessary shampooing her hair and shaving her legs because the view of the birds diving for breakfast among the sparkling waves entranced her. She could stand there all day if she had the time. She put her wet hair up in a puffy white towel and wrapped herself in the pink gingham Draper James robe she'd received as a bridal shower gift from Cristie.

Tally padded into the kitchen to make coffee and was pleased to see that most of the previous night's mess had been cleaned up. She'd loaded the dishwasher before bed and somebody else had emptied it during the night. Probably Rita, she had trouble sleeping. The Roomba she and Mitch had received as a wedding gift had also done its job, and she made a mental note to empty it and start it again when they left the house.

Tally hadn't wanted to take the robot vacuum out of its box because she believed it was bad luck to use gifts before the wedding day. She told all of her clients that, too. But her future sister-in-law had insisted that they open the Roomba immediately and name it – every Durham family had one and they all were named after television housekeepers or butlers. Robin swore it would be life-changing in their oceanfront house where you could always feel some sand under bare feet, no matter how hard they tried to keep the floors clean.

Mitch and Tally decided to keep it simple and called their Roomba "Alice" from "The Brady Bunch." Mitch sat down and actually read the entire instruction booklet, which Tally found highly amusing. He'd been running the new vacuum daily and playing with some of the features in the app that allowed him to start it remotely. He seemed to enjoy following Alice around the house – told Tally he was "busy vacuuming" – when he was home.

Tally wasn't really a fan of Alice, but she hadn't complained because he was taking his role as their household gadget guy seriously and she didn't want to discourage him. Whatever it took to make the beautiful beach house feel like home to Mitch was okay with Tally. The completion of The

Armory to hold his guns, uniforms, and gear had been a major step. Mitch seemed to settle in quickly after that was finished.

Thinking about Mitch, Tally looked at her watch and chuckled. He'd be on the golf course with his brothers because somebody had scheduled a ridiculously early tee time. Pete had promised that he'd build in some nap time in the afternoon before their rehearsal dinner, meaning they didn't plan to get their little brother too drunk because he had to get up in the morning to go shooting. She knew Pete's plan had nothing to do with the rehearsal dinner. Fortunately, she had Robin to keep an eye on things on that end, Tally hoped. Her sister-in-law had texted her a day earlier to confirm that she'd picked up all of the guys' dress uniforms from the dry cleaner. Tally was fighting the urge to call her and double check a few things when Cristie wandered out onto the deck with her own cup of coffee.

Chapter 38

"Whatcha doing?" Cristie asked, eyeing the clipboard on Tally's lap.

"Nothing."

"Liar," Cristie called her out, and then snatched the stack of lists out of Tally's hands. She set the clipboard on the deck railing, far enough away that Tally couldn't grab it, and then settled in the lounge chair beside Tally's.

"How'd you sleep?" Tally asked.

"Like a rock. You can really hear the waves with the windows open."

"I know, I love that. Mitch and I battle because he prefers air conditioning, but when it's this breezy out, I'd rather have windows open. I love that we can do that this week while he's not here," she said.

"Tally's learning to compromise," Cristie chuckled. "I know that's a struggle for you."

"Oh, shut up, I'm not that bad. Anymore... I've grown up a little bit," she defended herself, but then started giggling again. Cristie had known Tally for most of her life and there was absolutely no bullshitting her. Plus, they'd been roommates through several rotations at St. Margaret's and Cristie knew exactly how stubborn Tally could be.

"I'm trying not to freak out," Tally admitted. "I have nothing to freak out about but I am. My head has been spinning since yesterday."

"Your head has been spinning as long as I've known you, it's just spinning faster this week. Kinda scary to watch. You gotta figure out a way to slow yourself down or we're going to need pharmaceuticals for you soon." Cristie was only half joking because Tally looked wired and she was not a morning person. Something had her looking like that just past sunrise.

"Let's go for a beach walk," Cristie stood up and extended a hand to Tally.

"We're in pajamas."

"So what? You don't have any clients on the island."

Tally couldn't argue the point, so she got up from her lounge chair to follow her friend.

"Leave your cell phone here," Cristie ordered. "I've got mine if the world blows up. But you need 30 minutes without yours."

Tally wanted to argue but she knew that Cristie was right. It didn't mean she liked it, but she also wasn't going to fight. A beach walk would be restorative, right? If not, it would make her even more crazy and they could come back and figure out another strategy for keeping Tally off the ledge.

Chapter 39

Mitch leaned back against the railing on the front deck of The Wharf late that night and watched in awe as Tally and her girlfriends took over the dance floor to Billy Joel's "Only the Good Die Young." Every one of them was belting out the words at full volume as they danced together. Several of the girls had released deafening squeals after the band played the first few notes, then they'd rushed the dance floor en masse. The song had been on Tally's "must play" wish list that Mitch had shared with the band – all guys that he and Pete had known since high school – and now Mitch understood why. He looked around and saw that everybody else had also stopped what they were doing to watch the bridal party dance and sing. Quite a few people were holding up phones to film the girls.

He had a feeling that Tally wasn't going to be feeling very well the next morning. He'd never seen her quite like this before, at least not in public. The thought made him rethink having another cocktail. He had to go shooting at the crack of dawn with his brothers and if he had a headache, he'd be screwed. Tommy, Frank, and Pete would show him no mercy.

The actual wedding rehearsal on the lawn that afternoon had been in-formal, given that almost everybody there worked in the bridal business or had been in too many weddings to count. Even so, Kayla led them through who was walking with whom, and the boys were told where and how to stand (close together on an angle and not with any hands in pockets). Tally carried a massive ribbon bouquet that Yaya had made from the ribbons on the gifts at both of her bridal showers and the bride acted as silly as everybody else. Mitch had a much better time than he thought he would, based on stories he'd heard about Tally's clients' rehearsals.

Cheryl was the maid of honor, so she was walking down the aisle with his brother, Pete, who was Mitch's best man. His older brothers, Frank and Tommy, were escorting Yaya and Cristie. Joe Moody, the only one on Mitch's side that he wasn't related to, was partnered with Abby. Tally asked Abby to be matron of honor first, but Abby deferred because she was pregnant, and worried she wouldn't have time to take care of the MOH responsibilities because her due date was close to Tally's wedding date. Tally was just happy Abby was able to be part of the wedding at all because, from the look of things, she was overdue to give birth. Mitch had thought Cheryl was probably the best choice for maid of honor that any bride could hope for all along, because she was a wedding planner, too. She wouldn't miss a trick.

All of the men would wear their dress uniforms for the wedding ceremony. Tally had worried a little bit about the three different agencies' uniforms looking dumb in the pictures. When she mentioned it to Mitch, he jokingly called her a "bridezilla" and she hadn't said another word about it. He'd made a mental note to store that word away in case he ever needed to use it again. The look on Tally's face had been priceless.

The wedding officiant was also in uniform because he was the state police chaplain. Father Edwin Brown was a retired Episcopal priest who had been friends with the Durham family for longer than Tally and Mitch had been alive. He would be wearing a black vestment for their actual wedding ceremony, but for the rehearsal, he'd dressed in his police chaplain gear.

He'd refused any compensation from the couple for performing the ceremony, so Tally had cufflinks made with the Georgia State Patrol patch, and Father Brown's monogram, as a thank-you gift. They planned to give them to him after the rehearsal dinner and make a donation to a blue line charity in his name.

Mitch marveled daily over the little details Tally had taken care of for their wedding weekend. She'd mentioned most of it to him at some point in the process, but he didn't listen in a way that he retained what she was talking about when the item from the to-do list popped up finished on the actual wedding weekend.

For example, he'd been blown away a week ago when he got home and walked into a living room full of boxes.

"Are we moving?" he asked Tally, who was busy sorting something on a folding table she'd set up over the coffee table next to the couch.

"No, you goofball. I'm stuffing the welcome bags for our out-of-town wedding guests," she said and then finished counting something before she turned to him. "How was your day?"

"Obviously not as much fun as yours. Where did all of this come from?" he asked, mystified by its sudden appearance. There had to be at least 25 boxes. And they were big. He saw boxes of giant inflatable alligators in one of them.

"I've been stashing it, a box at a time, on the shelves in the garage."

"This garage?" The only things in the cinder block garage beneath the beach house were lawn tools and beach supplies.

"Yeah, there was an empty shelf and most of it has only been down there a few weeks. I just started shipping it directly here, and bringing what came in through the shop one box at a time. The hardest part was getting it all upstairs and in here, but I shanghaied Kayla and Yaya to help me this morning and we passed it up across the yard onto the side porch," she explained, gesturing with her arms.

"Do you need my help with anything?" he asked, half-wishing she'd say no but knowing she was up to her neck in a project that was for him, too.

"Nah, I got this. But you can help me put welcome packets together to stick into the bags later tonight. I have it all printed out, we just need to collate, staple, and stuff," she explained without missing a beat as she put beer cozies with their wedding date on them into each bag.

The tote bags were fancy-pants. Tally had agonized over them. She'd ordered so many different kinds of welcome bags, for so many different clients' weddings, and said she hadn't loved any of them. She really wanted to have "Jekyll Island" stitched on heavy-duty totes from Land's End or L.L. Bean, but they cost a lot more than the other options.

"Aren't these just for the out of towners?" Mitch had asked when he saw Tally flipping through the catalogs for the umpteenth time.

"Yes. Well, also for the wedding party."

"Then just get the bags you like and be done with it. I don't want you to regret your decision after you've bought something you hate," he told her.

Tally showed him the numbers and he had to use self-control not to react to the total she was spending for fewer than 50 bags, but the look on her face when he told her to go ahead and order the totes made them worth the overtime he'd need to work to pay for the upgrade.

She had all the bags filled by the time Mitch had showered and eaten something, and they assembled the welcome letters together on the dining room table. Then they added them to the bags. Tally had taken over the stuffing end of it because Mitch kept spotting neat things in the bags and taking them out to play with. And she didn't seem to have any sense of humor about it, in his opinion.

"You are way too easily distracted by shiny things," she said as she took a squirt gun out of his hand. "The extra stuff is in a box over there," she pointed. "You can play with that. Keep your paws out of the finished bags or people won't get everything they're supposed to."

"Is there extra beer?" he asked, ignoring her and pulling a six-pack made by Jekyll Brewing out of a bag. "You know these are actually brewed in Alpharetta?"

Tally resisted the urge to yank the beer out of Mitch's hand – she would have to empty the bag and start over because, obviously, the cans needed to be on the bottom or they'd crush the bags of salted caramel Beaver Nuggets from Buc-ees.

Mitch saw her face, even though she didn't say a word, and started to put the beer back.

"Just give it to me," she caught the six-pack before it landed on top of the delicate vanilla shortbread straw cookies she'd specially ordered for her guests from Jekyll Market. "I'll take care of this from here."

When Mitch looked disappointed, Tally gave her fiancé another assignment to get him out of her hair. He recognized it for what it was but took the orders like a champ.

"Actually, I do need your help. There are some boxes in the back of the Jeep that still need to be brought in here so I can finish making the special welcome bags for all the members of the wedding party," she explained.

"They get more than this?" Mitch was incredulous. "What else?"

"Beach towels and wine and a few other little things. Why? You jealous?" she teased. "Don't worry – I'm making one up for our room, too." She grinned as she told him this and Mitch smiled back at her even though he didn't get it.

It made zero sense to Mitch, who didn't think they actually *needed* any of the things his fiancée had listed. But he wasn't going to argue. Not only was Tally his bride, she was also a wedding planner. And she didn't try to tell him how to clean his guns.

Chapter 40

Tally's wedding day arrived earlier than it was supposed to. She'd brought her dress home from Aunt Etah's bridal shower; the hair stylist and make-up artist were coming to the house at noon, so she wasn't supposed to need to go anywhere before she left for the wedding.

When Tally and Cheryl had planned it out, sleeping late on her wedding day sounded great. But now that the big day was upon them, Tally couldn't sleep. She had approximately seven hours to kill before the planned activities started, and she was questioning everything.

Cristie found Tally on the front deck, watching the very start of sunrise over the Atlantic Ocean.

"I got up to get a bottle of water. Why are you up? You should be trying to sleep off last night," she told Tally.

"I feel okay."

"Then you're probably still drunk. No way you won't be feeling those shots we did – what the hell were we thinking – good thing we actually ate dinner before we really drank. Did you throw up?" she asked, making a face.

Tally considered lying but didn't bother.

"Oh yeah. More than once. But that's probably what's going to save me today. I can't believe I did that to myself," she whined.

"But we had fun."

"Oh my God, we sure did. That was a total blast. I'm so glad we had the band last night – I bet we won't get to do half as much dancing tonight," Tally said.

"Is that the kind of thing you're worrying about out here?" her friend laughed aloud at her. "Tally, you should really go back to bed for a few more hours. I don't want to sound mean, but you actually do need to try to get some beauty sleep. This is probably the only day in your life when it will actually make a difference. You will never spend this much money on pictures of yourself ever again."

It sounded like a speech Tally would have given an anxious bride, and that made her start giggling.

"I'm bridezilla, aren't I?"

"Not yet, but if you don't get a few more hours of sleep, I have a feeling you'll be a nightmare later," Cristie told her honestly.

"Ouch," Tally made a face.

"Truth hurts. I'm going back to bed. You should, too. I'll see you in the actual morning," Cristie blew Tally a kiss and headed back into the house.

Tally needed to write. She hadn't been blogging because she had signed off for the duration of her wedding festivities, but that writing functioned as a sort of cathartic journal for her and she was missing it. Instead of going back to sleep, she went back inside and found her laptop. She took it into the master bedroom with her and shut the door. Then she sat down on the bed and wrote a blog entry about how she was feeling. She had no plans to publish it until later, but it might be a fun way to kick off her post-wedding post, along with some of the pictures.

***

On the other side of the causeway in Brunswick, Mitch was being dragged out of a warm bed by his older brothers around the same time Tally was falling back asleep in their bed at home.

Robin had gotten up to make them a big breakfast before they headed to their friend's outdoor shooting range, but Pete didn't look like he was going to be able to eat anything. He was green. Frank and Tommy were a little worse for the wear, but nothing like Pete. Mitch was relieved because that likely meant his older brothers would focus on harassing the miserably hungover Pete all day instead of aggravating him.

Chapter 41

It was weird to be the one sitting in the chair and watching in the mirror as the heirloom veil was attached to her headpiece. The elaborate comb, and the veil it anchored to her golden curls, had been worn by generations of Durham brides. Yaya had used the comb to pull back the front of Tally's hair but left the back down.

"So help me, Tally, if I catch you tying your hair in a knot at your reception," she called out the bride's bad habit, "I'm going to spank you in front of everybody."

"I was just asking if somebody could bring a scrunchie to the reception for me," Tally whined.

"You're the bride tonight, remember?" Yaya's tone was firm. "You are not going to look like a frustrated secretary for your wedding pictures. If your hair is looking crazy, I'll tell you and I'll fix it. But keep your hands out of it. That just makes it bigger."

"It's a habit."

"I'm well aware."

Tally had woken up from her morning nap in a far perkier mood than she'd been in at sunrise.

"I think I was still drunk the first time I woke up this morning," she admitted.

"Even with puking, I don't know how you couldn't still be a little drunk now," Cristie said.

"Did I get sloppy before or after the grownups left the party?" Tally asked, not really wanting to know the answer.

"After," Yaya replied.

Abby and Todd left the party shortly after the rehearsal dinner because Abby was feeling 10 months pregnant. The other women got her caught her up on the shenanigans she'd missed.

"Tally wasn't that bad," Rita defended the bride. "She was just super happy and loved everybody. She loves all of us, all of Mitch's friends, all of the bartenders, all of the servers..."

"Oh God," Tally held up a hand to hide her face. "I didn't."

"Oh, you did. But you were cute. You're never a bitchy drunk, you just get really, really loud," Rita said.

"I don't think anybody could really hear you anyway once the guys started hooting and hollering," Yaya said, as she carefully detached the veil and passed it back over to the other girls to hang up.

"Poor Mitch," Tally sighed, but she couldn't keep the smirk off her face.

"Yeah, I think his brothers should have waited til after their parents left before they threw Mitch in the river. His dad was really mad," Rita reported. "I thought he was going to push Mitch's brothers off the dock for a minute there."

Roberta had saved the day – or her sons' butts, at least – by taking her husband by the arm and leading him up the dock and away from their sons, who had started performing cannonballs with some of the other party guests. Most of the idiots participating in the splashing were cops so nobody was going to get in trouble.

Chapter 42

Tally and Mitch had opted to keep their ceremony décor very simple because the historic hotel's pretty lawn had the river on one side of it and the Jekyll Island Club Hotel on the other. No matter what angle the wedding photographers were shooting from, the background would be spectacular.

There were black iron tiki torches burning at the outer end of each row of chairs, and the blue ribbons tied to them (an exact match to the bridesmaid dress color) fluttered gently in the light breeze. The torches weren't decorative – they were absolutely necessary. Sunset was when the mosquitos and no-see-ums came out and attacked. The citronella oil burning in the torches surrounding the ceremony would serve as a bug forcefield for all but the most tender of bait.

The guests were on time, and so were the groomsmen, thanks to heroic efforts by Robin to get the Durham men cleaned up, dressed up, and loaded into her minivan on schedule. Tally had put a note on her "Things To Do After The Wedding" list reminding herself to get her sister-in-law a special thank you present.

The guests could see Tally from a distance as she crossed the big lawn on her soon-to-be father-in-law's arm. Tom was wearing his dress uniform, too, and they cut quite an image.

She carried a big, fluffy bouquet of pink peonies, and she held it low so they wouldn't block the top of her gown, the way she coached her clients.

"Crotch flowers," she reminded herself in a whisper, using the phrase she used with bridal parties at rehearsal.

Mitch's dad heard her and stopped walking.

"What did you say?"

Tally laughed and urged them on. "I said crotch flowers. That's how we remember to hold them super low for pictures."

"Always the wedding planner," Tom chuckled.

They were getting closer, and Tally could see Mitch waiting for her at the end of the aisle and hear the guitarist playing "Puff the Magic Dragon." It wasn't a traditional processional, and they'd kept it instrumental, but the bride and groom both vividly remembered singing that song together, over and over again, on the beach when they were little kids. Using it in the wedding had been Mitch's bright idea. Aunt Etah was grinning at her from the most important seat in the house, where the mother of the bride usually sat. She'd recognized the song for what it was and was enjoying every second of it.

Everybody else Tally loved was there waiting for her, too. But she had tunnel vision for the handsome man grinning at her, and it took some self-control not to speed up to an unladylike pace and race down the aisle to Mitch.

When they reached the first row of chairs, Tom stopped and Mitch approached them, just as they'd rehearsed. Tom kissed Tally on the cheek and shook his son's hand. And then he put Tally's hand in Mitch's hand and stepped away to the empty seat saved for him next to his wife. His job was done. Since Tally's parents were dead, the couple had opted to entirely omit the section of the ceremony where Father Brown would have traditionally asked "who gives this man" and "who gives this woman."

"It's outdated anyway," the elderly man had assured them when they met with him to plan the service. "Nobody is giving this bright young woman away. She is making her own decision. As is Mitch."

"Good, thank you," Tally said.

"We can cut out the part where you promise to obey him too, if you'd like," Father Brown suggested.

"You can leave that in," Mitch interrupted the priest. "It's hard enough to keep her out of trouble without giving her permission to ignore me."

Tally giggled and Father Brown raised an eyebrow at them. They both noticed with amusement that the word "obey" was omitted from the vows on their wedding day.

The ceremony whizzed by – at least in Tally's memory later on. Neither of them believed in long, weird ceremony traditions, but they did perform a sand-blending ceremony. Tally held a cruet of black sand from that famous beach on Vieques Island, and Mitch's container held sugary white sand from Glory Beach. They poured them, in layers, into a bottle they would cork and keep someplace special in their home. It symbolized the merging of their lives.

Chapter 43

"You're just determined to break all of the rules, aren't you?" Kayla teased as she took a glass out of Tally's hand so the photographer could snap a photo. "You tell all your clients to refrain from serving drinks to the wedding party until after pictures but you and Mitch had them bring a mini bar onto the lawn for pictures. Hypocrite!"

Isabelle stood to the side, laughing hysterically at the scene. She had a cane to give her extra balance on the grassy lawn, but for a lady who'd broken her hip and ankle not so long ago, she was walking really well. Tally had been thrilled her friend felt steady enough to come be part of her wedding. It wouldn't have been right without Isabelle there. Without her support in transitioning all the disrupted Vieques weddings to Jekyll Island, Tally might not have a successful wedding planning company anywhere.

Kayla wasn't wrong in her accusation. Tally had been breaking all of her own rules. The rules she'd created herself to keep things running smoothly for clients. But Tally justified her actions by telling herself she knew the consequences of her actions before she did any of the things she forbid other couples to do. It made sense in her head.

Their cocktail hour was held on the front lawn of the historic hotel, on and beside the croquet court. They'd been inspired to do it there (someplace she'd never done somebody else's cocktails) after seeing a picture of an event held there by the millionaires in the early 1900s, when it was still the "Golden Age" at the Jekyll Island Club.

There were always a few benches and tables with umbrellas beside the court for spectators. Tally had added additional seating and some high-boy tables. Her bridesmaids carried lace parasols that matched their dresses, a silly expenditure that Tally hadn't been able to resist once she got the idea in her head. The scene was straight out of *The Great Gatsby*.

Tally had planned more than 20 events in the Grand Dining Room of the Jekyll Island Club Hotel, but it had never looked like the way it did on her wedding night. No bride in the history of Jekyll could have ever had as many gorgeous flowers as Tally. Candles flickered on every tabletop and the chandeliers overhead were dimmed. To the right, inside the entrance to the dining room, Yaya had constructed the most over-the-top flower wall that Tally had ever seen. It had been created to serve as a backdrop for the informal photo booth but looked like so much more than that. Tally knew that it must have taken her friend hours – on top of all the bouquets and centerpieces and everything else she'd been working on for Tally and Mitch's wedding.

As a general rule, Tally wasn't a fan of flower walls. Most people used carnations to fill the bulk of the space and she didn't like the way it looked. But Yaya's wall of peonies, pink oriental lilies, hydrangeas, and garden roses in shades from white to deep pink, was nothing like anything Tally had ever seen in person. It looked like a magazine cover with a puffy pile of flowers you could throw yourself on. She wondered how many flower tubes were anchored to the back of it to keep such delicate blooms alive.

The centerpieces were pink and white peonies and roses in short, eight-inch square black cube vases. Tally had wanted to keep everything low – she hated it when she couldn't see her dinner partners over the flowers. Each vase had a thin blue ribbon tied around it. Another nod to the presence of her new law enforcement family in the room. The taper candles that Yaya had found were ivory with thin ribbons of blue and there were several burning on every table.

Chapter 44

Tally didn't remember eating dinner at her reception because she'd spent most of it going from table to table thanking everyone for coming to the wedding. Several times, Mitch had appeared at her elbow to lead her back to her seat when the next course was served.

"Sit down and eat," Mitch told her after the third time he'd retrieved her. "I'm getting lonely."

That was unlikely given that the rest of their table was made up of his brothers and their immediate families and everybody was having a great time, but Tally got the underlying message.

"I'm not trying to ignore you. I'm sorry for that," she began. "But I really want to relax and party after dinner and with no receiving line, that meant I needed to say hello to everybody while they were seated so I could keep track and not miss anybody."

"You are clinically insane."

"Probably."

"I love you anyway," Mitch said, leaning in for a kiss. The guests caught them in the act and began banging silverware on their wine glasses to encourage more smooches. The result was the reverse.

"Oh my God, I hate that," Tally muttered to Mitch as she kept a big smile pasted on her face. He knew. She'd ranted more than once about how guests would break glasses and centerpieces by whacking them.

"Well, you'd better ignore it because I'm not going to stop kissing you," Mitch told her.

"You better not. I want you to kiss me over and over again every day for the rest of our lives."

Isabelle took the microphone when it was time for the toasts and acted as a master of ceremonies. Aunt Etah went first and she kept her speech brief.

"Tally, I couldn't be prouder of the woman you've become, or happier about the man you've chosen to be your life partner. Having you as my daughter was an unexpected blessing. My life is richer with you in it, and I know the Durham family feels the same way. It makes me so happy to know that one day, when I'm gone, you will still have this big loving family around you," she stopped to take a deep breath. Then she raised her glass in the air.

"To Mitch and Tally, may you continue to find treasure in your lives every day on Jekyll Island. Congratulations!" She took a sip and there were calls of "here, here!" from the guests. Tally rushed to her aunt to give her a hug and a kiss and was struck by how thin and fragile Etah felt. She was in her 80s but to Tally, she never aged. Her energy certainly hadn't flagged.

Mitch's family's toasts were next, and each of his brothers was worse than the man before him. Nobody told any lewd stories, but it was clear nobody was going to let their baby brother off the hook easily, either. Roberta put an end to it when Tommy's toast went on too long – despite the fact that the guests and the bridal couple were laughing hysterically – and handed the microphone to her husband. Tom welcomed Tally to the family in "an official capacity" claiming he hadn't learned they weren't related to her until she'd started dating Mitch.

"She was always around when she was little, and then she was here when she was not so little. I yelled at her when she got into mischief with my sons. I yelled at my older boys when they teased her mercilessly. Tally has always been a part of our family. Now it's legal, too," he announced.

Roberta went last. Mitch's mom turned out to be the funniest toast of the night. She'd been up to something, Tally could tell by the way her mother-in-law signaled to Kayla and Yaya before she faced the guests to toast.

"Does anybody need more champagne? Because this is going to take a minute," the mother of the groom began with an impish grin. "Tally, I apologize. I know you hate surprises, but he's my last baby to get married and I put together something special to show you. If you'd all look that direction..." Roberta pointed toward the far wall, where a screen was slowly descending from the ceiling. Then the room went dark and the slideshow of Mitch and Tally growing up together began. Roberta narrated.

The first picture was of them as infants in onesies – Tally had a lot of hair and Mitch was bald. Roberta was holding Mitch, and Tally's mother was holding her. Tally had to take a deep breath as she felt the tears welling up inside her. Roberta had found a way to have Tally's parents at her wedding, and she would be forever grateful. Even if the gesture had broken the cardinal rule by surprising her.

The baby pictures Roberta used were pretty hilarious, and Tally knew Etah and Bonnie had done a lot of digging to help put it together. The biggest laughs were of the shots of Tally and Mitch, naked as jaybirds, in a wading pool on Etah's deck, while their parents sat in chairs around them holding cocktails. There were also pictures of them naked on the beach, naked in Bonnie's backyard, naked on somebody's boat, and naked in the bathtub together. One of the guests finally yelled "didn't they have clothes?"

There was a picture of Tally and Mitch, probably at age 3, hanging onto the back of the golf cart with a barely teenage Tommy driving. No seatbelts.

"Don't judge," Roberta told her viewing audience. "The rules were different then. They're all still alive now so I don't want to hear about it. The grandchildren are strapped in."

The slideshow spun picture after picture of the two families growing up. All of the summertime shots of the Durham children included Tally, usually standing next to Mitch. Or floating next to him as the kids formed a giant flotilla of innertubes and rafts in the water in front of Etah's house. Eventually, pictures showed she got to be the top of the human pyramid because she was the smallest. The pictures also revealed that, after her parents died, Tally joined their family photos year-round.

Roberta had blessedly ended her surprise slideshow with their high school graduations, making it unnecessary to explain the 10-year gap that ensued in their friendship.

"Tally, when you were little, I always thought I'd have loved to have a daughter like you. I was so jealous of your mom, the way she'd change your outfit four times a day like you were a baby doll. I feel like we've come full circle, and God decided that I deserved to have you as my daughter after all, but in an even better way. Because I know with certainty that you are going to make Mitch blissfully happy for the rest of this life," she ended the toast, raising her glass in the air.

Chapter 45

Isabelle invited the bride and groom to the dance floor for "their first official dance as husband and wife" as soon as the applause for Roberta died down. They'd played down the last-name stuff in all their wedding events because Tally wasn't planning to take Mitch's name professionally. She'd be Mrs. Durham when she was with him, and Miss Tally to the neighborhood kids, because that's how they did it in the South. But Tally Davis had earned her own spot in the wedding world and her name was recognizable now. It didn't bother Mitch in the slightest. Tally wanted their kids to have his last name.

Tally and Mitch had chosen an unusual song for their first dance at their wedding, but she didn't care. She'd always thought brides were ridiculous when they banned every anti-love song from their playlists, but even she had to admit they were pushing the limits with their selection. She hoped nobody would ask about it.

The song, "Follow Me" by Uncle Kracker, was about infidelity, but that wasn't what it meant to Mitch and Tally. The song's lyrics "I'll be the one to tuck you in at night," harkened back to the early days of their romantic relationship when Mitch would slide into Tally's house when he was on duty to kiss her goodnight. They'd danced to it a hundred times in their own living room in the months before their wedding but didn't think they needed to waste money on lessons. She reminded Mitch about Tonya's tantrum on the dance floor when Ronald goofed on their carefully-orchestrated steps and told her own fiancé that she just wanted them to have fun and not look too stupid.

"Let's just have a good time with it," she told Mitch. She explained about how her own feet would be hidden, so it didn't really matter what she did as long as she looked like she was floating in his arms.

They looked better than that on their wedding night. A few cocktails had loosened Mitch up, and he surprised his bride by dipping her more than once; she looked adorable in his arms and the pictures would show they'd been having a blast.

When their song ended, the music immediately switched tone and the Black Eyed Peas "I Gotta Feeling" began blasting from the speakers. The desired result was immediate – guests filled the dance floor and those who were still sitting down, got up. The DJ took them through a whole gamut of music from Jimmy Buffett to AC/DC and the dance floor stayed full. There were no line dances. The Michael Jackson and Grease mixes were banned. Songs like "Bad Boys" and "I Fought the Law" were bracketed by Spice Girls and the Go-Go's.

Tally didn't sit down once the whole time, but Mitch took a number of breaks. He enjoyed watching her with her girlfriends. They acted so silly when they got together. He would make a point to suggest that they travel to visit Abby and Todd and everybody else up in the DC area soon. It was easy to expect people to want to come to the beach to visit, but Mitch owed it to Tally to try to learn more about where she was from and get to know her best friends better. His father danced with Etah and Bonnie and Robin and Tally before spending most of his time dancing with Mitch's mom. Roberta was in her element and they were having the time of their lives.

All of the wedding professionals who had made their event come together spent most of the night dancing, too. Mayra and Kayla danced with each other, and the DJ, before Tommy and Frank dragged them to the center of the dance floor during "Time of My Life" from "Dirty Dancing."

Tally visited the ladies' room before the cake cutting and tried to put herself back together.

"I'm nasty sweaty all over," she complained to Kayla, who came along to help her make sure she didn't pee on her dress. "Sorry you have to do this."

"Oh Tally, we hold dresses in the bathroom for every bride. At least I know and love you. Besides, you have to do this for me someday," Kayla said.

"I would be honored," Tally joked.

She washed her hands and used a paper towel to gently pat the sweat off her face, trying not to remove what remained of her makeup.

"You want your lipstick?" Kayla asked, holding out Tally's evening bag.

"Do I have to? Mitch hates getting goo all over his lips."

"Nah, skip it. You have plenty of shots with perfect makeup from earlier. Don't want to discourage kissing on your wedding night." Then Kayla started laughing and couldn't stop.

"Do you realize that you just asked me for permission to not do something at your own wedding? This is priceless," she said once she caught her breath.

"I did," Tally admitted.

"You're finally acting like a bride. C'mon," Kayla pulled open the door of the ladies' room. "Let's go find Yaya. She's going to think this is as funny as I do."

Chapter 46

Their wedding cake was a white chocolate mousse cake, frosted entirely in white chocolate shavings. It wasn't what Tally thought she wanted but Mitch fell in love with it at the tasting. Tally thought the white chocolate mousse tasted heavenly, but she knew it was tricky to work with because each layer was heavy and delicate. Mitch hadn't voiced many preferences in the planning so she felt like letting him pick the cake was the right thing to do.

The pastry chef had wanted to put the tiers on columns for support, but Tally hated that look. They compromised by keeping it a two-tier cake (they'd have sheet cakes in the kitchen to serve, too) and the chef promised to hide supports in the first tier that wouldn't be noticeable.

Everything on the beautiful cake was edible, including the very real-looking wide black ribbon with a thin blue line through it that ran around the middle of each tier. Most brides would have probably put the ribbon at the bottom, but Tally wanted it to be clear and obvious to all the members of law enforcement there that the detail was intentional. It was subtle but beautiful and somehow, it just worked. She loved her cake and almost felt guilty cutting into it.

Mitch behaved like a perfect gentleman when they cut the cake, and carefully fed a bite to his bride. Tally got a little messy feeding him, but he would hold his revenge for later that night. It made for cute pictures and everybody raved when they took their first bite.

"Oh my Lord, this is fantastic," Etah crowed when she tasted it. "I want this for every birthday for the rest of my life. It's amazing." She shoved another big bite into her mouth.

"We're not quite done with cake," Tally whispered to her aunt. "It's time to surprise Mitch."

Just as she said it, the music stopped and the DJ switched to a drumroll. The doors to the main dining room opened. Several uniformed state patrol troopers entered, pushing a rolling table into the room. On top of it stood a four-foot tall Krispy Kreme donut cake. There were more donuts on platters on the cake table with paper Krispy Kreme napkins displayed beside them.

***

Mitch thought the donut cake was fantastic. He shoved two of the donuts he'd nicknamed "Power Rings" into his mouth, one after the other. There was no Krispy Kreme anywhere near Jekyll Island but he'd gotten addicted to the sugary treats when he was living in Atlanta. He *had to* stop if the "hot" sign in the window was lit up when he passed. Mitch knew somebody had gone to a great effort to deliver his favorite treat to their wedding reception and once again, he was awed by his fiancée's – no wait, they were married now – his wife's creativity.

Mitch and his groomsmen posed for multiple pictures with the donut cake. Then they posed with their bosses – who were all guests at the wedding – as the officials loaded their own plates with several donuts apiece. Tally had a feeling some of those snaps would end up on the "Wall of Shame" she'd seen in the barrack's conference room.

Chapter 47

"This has been the perfect night," Mitch told Tally as they swayed together on the dance floor a little later.

"Shush," Tally put a finger on Mitch's lips. "Do not jinx us. This isn't over yet."

"It's almost over," Mitch let go of Tally to look at his watch. "Only another 20 minutes. Wow, that went by really fast. Now I know why you added an hour to the reception budget from the beginning."

"Yeah, well. I've listened to 100 brides whine when the party ended. I didn't want to feel like that. But I still do. This has been a really amazing night," she said. "Thank you for marrying me."

Mitch laughed. "Me? Thank *you* for marrying me! You're the best thing that has ever happened to me."

They were still dancing together a few songs later when the DJ announced it was time for the last dance. The song they'd chosen to use was another unexpected tune at a wedding, and another nod to the cops in attendance.

"Bye Bye, Miss American Pie" was the unofficial law enforcement anthem at the end of events, not unlike Semisonic's "Closing Time" at a bar. When the first notes of the song began playing, every officer and their family members rushed the dance floor to participate in the tradition. Tally had heard about it but had never seen it before. She'd trusted Mitch's judgement when he'd made the suggestion and couldn't have been more pleased with the result.

Everybody was singing and dancing to the song, with the girls spinning around the dance floor together again. When Don McLean got to the line "This'll be the day that I die," at the end of each chorus, more than a hundred voices shouted "Bullshit!" at the top of their lungs, every time.

Afterwards, Kayla stood by the doors, pointing the favor table out to everyone who walked past it on their way out. Each guest received a Thin Blue Line-printed bag filled with freshly baked chocolate chip cookies. Sitting beside the cookies, on ice, were little, single-serving milk bottles. Mitch had known that Tally was doing cookies as favors, but he hadn't known about the theme or the milk.

"She gotcha, didn't she?" his father asked, giving Tally a fist bump.

"He deserved it, didn't he?" she winked at him.

"He did."

Tom turned to explain to one of his friends how Tally had caught his youngest son stealing cookies out of the bags that she'd asked him to give to his father and brothers. When Pete complained about only getting three cookies, Tally was confused. There were six big cookies in each bag when she handed them to Mitch.

Mitch eventually confessed he'd been charging his brothers a "delivery fee" out of each bag of cookies. It was dumb because there was a whole Tupperware of cookies sitting on their kitchen counter and he didn't need to steal. But after that, Tally gave Mitch a baggie of his own treats to eat while he made the deliveries so there would be no more shortages.

"I'm so freaking glad we decided not to throw a brunch tomorrow," Tally told Mitch softly in a break between hugging guests goodbye.

"Yeah, me too. I'm ready to get out of here. Do you want to change first?" he asked.

"Are you kidding? I never get to wear this dress again. I'm not changing until you take it off of me."

"Is that an invitation?" he asked, bending to kiss her on the neck.

"It's a suggestion. Let's get out of here," Tally tugged his hand and he followed. They stopped to kiss Aunt Etah and his parents goodbye and then made their way out to Mitch's truck, which had been preloaded with their luggage.

Tally stopped short at the top of the stairs and started laughing at Mitch's truck that the valet had waiting under the portico. Mitch's jaw dropped and he said nothing at all before his older brothers appeared behind him, laughing.

"It washes off, don't get all huffy," Tommy told him.

"Just Married" was written in pink all over the pickup truck, but that wasn't all. There were long trails of lace ribbon tied to everything they could find to tie them to, and lots of cans – tied with lace, of course – trailing on the ground behind the truck.

Tally could see Mitch trying to figure out how to react. She leaned in closer to her husband to whisper. "Just wait til we get away from the hotel and we can take it all off. Be a good sport."

He took her advice and they drove away laughing, with his brothers and their friends making quite a stir at the entrance. Tally felt sorry for the hotel guests who were not a part of their wedding and reminded Mitch not to honk.

They drove across the historic district dragging the cans, and then Mitch pulled into the first parking lot outside of the gates. He'd told Tally to stay in the truck because she was in her wedding gown, and she guided him through her suitcase in back to find scissors that would make removing all those ribbons in the dark much easier.

"Did you pack the kitchen sink?" Mitch joked.

"Do you want to use my scissors?" Tally retorted.

"Oops. I think I meant I hope you packed the kitchen sink in case we need it. I'm so glad you packed scissors."

"I'm sure you are." She sat quietly with a smile on her face for the five minutes it took Mitch to remove the wedding décor from their truck. A few guests had caught them – waving and hollering as they passed by – but nobody stopped, thank God.

When Mitch got back in the truck, Tally reached across the seat and pulled him to her for a deep, long kiss.

"Take me to bed. Now," she told him.

"Your wish is my command, Mrs. Durham," he replied. Tally giggled and slid back over to her seat as her husband put his truck in gear.

"We're going on a honeymoon," she said in a sing-song voice.

"I thought we were going to do that in a few months," Mitch argued.

"This is our mini-moon, but it's still a honeymoon. And I plan to take full advantage of being a newlywed on Sea Island for the next few days," she explained.

"Oh, so we're going to leave the room?" Mitch sounded disappointed.

"Well, I'd planned to... but maybe you can change my mind."

Epilogue

A Note from the Author:

Just in case you missed it in the disclaimers at the beginning the book, I intentionally ignored the fact that the pandemic shut down the world shortly before Tally and Mitch's wedding. When I thought about whether to include it in my story, I remembered feeling relieved when "Grey's Anatomy" decided to do their next season in an imaginary, post-pandemic world. I didn't want Tally's wedding to be ruined by Covid. I hope my readers understand.

May 2021

The world shut down for a period of time during Tally and Mitch's newlywed year due to the havoc wrought by the coronavirus pandemic. While it was scary, it was better going through it together. After the initial panic and shutdowns, Jekyll actually got busier.

Desperate tourists from places in lockdown sought sanctuary vacations in the more reasonable states like Georgia, and filled the hotels and rental houses. Jekyll Island's beaches never shut down. And since most of its restaurants already had outside seating, they did fine, too. Shops struggled a little to create larger outside displays for the masked northerners who were afraid to step inside. But for Tally and her team at Jekyll Weddings, the calendar went gangbusters.

Once the world re-opened, brides and grooms were afraid to ask their guests to leave the United States for destination weddings because there was a real chance they could get stuck trying to get home. The rules about when you had to be screened for Covid ahead of getting on a plane varied from country to country, and the horror stories on the news of people stuck in airports kept everyone who didn't have to get on a plane at home.

The coastal states of California, Oregon, New York, Massachusetts, New Jersey, Michigan, and Maryland had all made it nearly impossible to have a big wedding with the ordinances that were passed about how many people could occupy how many square feet. That took famously popular U.S. wedding destinations like Coronado, Napa, Martha's Vineyard, Mackinac Island, and Nantucket off the list. Even as far down as Virginia and South Carolina, the restrictions and rules were prohibitive. Event planning companies in those states struggled, or went out of business entirely, at the same time wedding planners along the coasts of Georgia, Florida, Alabama, and Texas got slammed. People didn't stop getting married because of the pandemic, they just changed up their destinations.

Tally didn't even need to spend money on advertising. It was like everybody who had never heard of Jekyll Island before Covid was drawn there at the same time, seeking the freedom of maskless beach walks. But after the beach walks, they got hungry and inevitably ended up wandering through Beach Village. Tally had installed a neat sign in the flower shop window that read, "Yes, we plan big maskless weddings!"

Kayla had been worried that the snarky sign would serve as a turn-off, but by the time Tally put it up, most people were over the whole pandemic thing and the sign made them laugh. Yaya tracked the walk-in wedding inquiries from that point on and said she thought they were getting at least 10 times as many a week as they had before the rest of the world shut down.

"I mean I wasn't formally tracking it a year ago so I can't compare May of 2019 to the same month in 2020, but I used to be able to get stuff done when I was working in here alone. And now there is always somebody at the counter asking about weddings or flowers for weddings. I'm telling you, Tally. Work in the office all day for a couple of weeks and you'll see," Yaya said.

Tally usually worked from her house unless Yaya needed her hands for a big flower order. Most of the time, Kayla and Tally met and worked together at the beach house, although Kayla's actual desk and office space were in the back of the flower shop. Like Tally, Kayla struggled to write contracts and confirm vendors when she was being interrupted every few minutes by people who popped in with questions.

Jekyll Flowers had grown by leaps and bounds because people were sending a lot of flowers to sick people. Tally had to buy a delivery van because the funeral arrangements were frequently too big for an SUV. Mitch found her an old prisoner transport vehicle that the Glynn County Sheriff's Office was auctioning off super cheap because the interior was basically an empty shell, and it needed a paint job.

The van sat in a parking spot in Beach Village for the first two days she had it while Mitch made arrangements to have it fixed up. On the third day, Mitch moved it over to his parents' house in Brunswick after the head of the Jekyll Island Authority called his father to suggest that the former sheriff's vehicle, which sported the warning "Stay Back, Prisoner Transport Vehicle," should be relocated to a place that wouldn't be seen by every single tourist who arrived on the island. The van was returned to its spot a couple of weeks later with four new tires and wrapped in Jekyll Flowers and Weddings logos. Yaya hired a part-time driver to make deliveries and told Tally that it wouldn't be long before they'd need to bump him up to full time.

St. Simons Island had really come into play for Jekyll Weddings during the pandemic because there weren't enough wedding planners on the bigger island to the north to handle the influx of potential clients. Brides who had traditionally used northern destination wedding planners were looking for local ones in the Golden Isles, and Tally's business boomed because of it.

At first, Tally and Kayla directed their clients to the bigger resorts and hotels on St. Simons and tried to avoid doing events in villas or private homes until they had more staff. A wedding at a hotel took a lot less manpower on the wedding planner's end. Regardless, always trying to split themselves between Jekyll and St. Simons for weddings at the same time was proving to be super difficult.

Kayla was ready to run things for Tally on St. Simons but Tally wasn't quite ready to pull the trigger on formally launching a company there with everything else she had coming in the next calendar year. She needed to replace Kayla on Jekyll before committing to a full wedding calendar on St. Simons Island, too.

When their first wedding anniversary arrived, Tally didn't try to make a big deal of it. Mitch was gone for three days on a task force mission right beforehand, but his boss promised he'd make it home to take his wife to dinner on May 30th.

He raced into the house on their anniversary not 10 minutes before they were due to leave. Driftwood Bistro didn't usually take reservations, but they'd kindly made an exception for the anniversary couple on holiday weekend, and Tally didn't want to be late. They had the best fried green tomatoes and she'd been thinking about them all day. Mitch would have the shrimp and grits because that's what he always got when they went there.

The hostess had saved them a small table off to the side, which gave them a little bit of cover and privacy. It had come to the point that they couldn't go anywhere on Jekyll without running into friends – and most of the time they absolutely loved it that way. But this was their first wedding anniversary and Tally wanted to celebrate with Mitch alone.

There was a bottle of champagne waiting for them – a gift from the owner – and the server opened it and poured them each a glass. Mitch asked for a whiskey sour and Tally ordered an Arnold Palmer.

"It's only a three-minute drive home, ya know," he joked. "We could walk it. Get a cocktail."

"I've already got champagne," she said, sipping from the bubbling glass with a smile. She wasn't much of a drinker unless she was with a group of girlfriends.

Their honeymoon was the dinner topic of the evening. The pandemic had screwed up both of their schedules – Mitch had spent a month working traffic control at a vaccination station in Atlanta – and neither of them was interested in sitting on an airplane in a mask for a long flight. Nor were they willing to get on a cruise ship after hearing about a friend's nightmare when her Holland America boat wasn't allowed to dock for weeks.

"I think we need to postpone it for another year," Tally told him. "I mean, we can take trips, but I don't want to remember our 'honeymoon' as the time we went to that great place where we had to wear masks at dinner except when we're eating."

Mitch nodded in understanding, but he was really trying to come up with someplace special they could go where it wouldn't be like that. He thought Tally deserved a break and calling a trip "the honeymoon" meant she wouldn't try to work while they traveled. But he hadn't gotten her to commit to any of the ideas he'd floated thus far.

"I don't think we should make any big travel commitments right now," Tally said, dashing his plans. "Things are going to get crazy around here over the next year. Crazier than they are already, I should say," she teased with a smile.

"Why? Have you decided to go ahead and open shop on St. Simons?" he asked.

"Nope. Because we're pregnant."

Acknowledgements

Thank you to Kayla Blunk, Kelsi Welch, Susan McLemore, Rita Rich, Cristie Farrar, Cathy Wilson, Christine Tippelmann, Ruthmary Williams, Shari Perez, Leigh Baughman, and Pamela Bauer Mueller for your amazing contributions to my writing and my spirit. Special thanks to my husband for taking on the roll of book delivery boy for our local shops. He says it's easier than wedding planning.

The credit for the beautiful cover design goes to Patti Tait of Gravitait Design. The beautiful photograph is the work of my friends David and Julie Fisher. Thank you for helping me.

About the Author

Sandy Malone is best known for starring in TLC's reality TV show "Wedding Island" and writing hundreds of wedding advice columns that were published in BRIDES, WeddingWire, and HuffPost. She wrote a DIY wedding planning book in 2016 that was traditionally published, and she released her new fiction series - Gem of the Golden Isles - in April 2024. She has also ghostwritten books for well-known reality TV stars (including a Real Housewife). Most recently, she was editor of The Police Tribune.

Sandy got her journalism degree at The Ohio State University and was a reporter and editor for major news publications before she returned to her hometown of Washington, DC, for a career in public relations and government affairs. She began planning destination weddings professionally after her own was nearly a disaster, and ended up planning more than 500 weddings in the Caribbean in 11 years with her retired SWAT-commander husband.

Sandy and her husband, Bill, recently moved to Jekyll Island, Georgia, with their coonhound Sherlock. "Treasure on Jekyll" is her third fiction novel in the Gem of the Golden Isles Series. Check out her website at www.SandyMalone.com.

Also by Sandy Malone

Escape to Jekyll Island – Gem of the Golden Isles Series Book One
Twenty-nine-year-old destination wedding planner Tally Davis lost her home, her job, and her boyfriend in one fell swoop when Hurricane Maria hit Vieques Island, Puerto Rico. After she's finally evacuated, she goes home to Jekyll Island, Georgia, to start over. There's no wedding planning company on the island, so Tally launches Jekyll Weddings. But not everyone is happy that Tally is home or wants her to succeed. She's unknowingly kicked a hornet's nest by reconnecting with a childhood friend. Will a 10-year-old grudge ruin her first big wedding on Jekyll Island?

In Bloom on Jekyll – Gem of the Golden Isles Series Book Two
Tally Davis reinvented herself after a hurricane left her homeless and jobless in Puerto Rico, and now she has survived her first year in the wedding planning on Jekyll Island. Bonus - she's in love with a hot state trooper she's known since childhood. She's ready to grow her business by opening a flower shop in Georgia when a former client turns up with an outrageous demand. Will Tally figure out how to rise above the chaos or will her past burn her future to the ground?

In the Shadows on Jekyll – Gem of the Golden Isles Series Book Four (Coming Soon!)

Tally Davis is a victim of her own success. Her wedding and flower businesses on Jekyll Island are going gangbusters when she's doubly-blessed with motherhood. She can't keep so many balls in the air for all of her brides and grooms without help. But as the team grows, so do her problems. Not everyone is who they appear to be when she hired them – some just want unfettered access to the island for nefarious purposes. Will her state trooper husband spot the problem before it kills both of their careers?

How To Plan Your Own Destination Wedding: Do-It-Yourself Tips From An Experienced Professional, Skyhorse Publishing 2016

Ten years ago, when Sandy was planning her own destination wedding in the Caribbean, she learned everything the hard way. After 11 years in business and more than 500 successfully executed weddings, she wrote a DIY guide that any wedding couple can follow to create a fabulous destination wedding for themselves anywhere.

Check out Sandy's blog and sign up for the newsletter at
www.SandyMalone.com
to find out about upcoming novels and book signings.